THE DRAGON'S PLEDGE

JADE DRAGON SHIFTER BROTHERS

MARIE JOHNSTON

LE PUBLISHING

Ronan

The next time my brother says "Hey, I've got an idea," I need to run, not walk away. I might be from a dragon shifter ruling family, but I'm not demanding a female mate with me. Yet taking my time and winning her over is going nowhere. So far, I've punched my card as the older neighbor who's way too nosy about the young female next door. Then I hear about what she's got planned. And I'm faced with giving her what she needs and letting her walk away, even at the cost of the useless beating organ in my chest.

Brighton

Mate Ronan Jade, they said. *It'll be a good match*, they said. The older shifter is a walking poster of smoldering, hardworking male. He swings a hammer all day and at night... Well, that thought dominates my mind more than I'd like. The problem is that he's a great match. Superb. And I'm an inexperienced female trying to rule my clan. It'd be too easy to let him in. To let him take over. To allow him to dominate. So I try to find another mate instead. Only Ronan finds me first.

B righton

I SCOWLED at the dating app. There had to be a decent prospect out there, but so far, all I'd gotten was three dick pics—not impressive ones either—a request to be a sugar baby, which I'd had to look up, and a guy who said he didn't like outspoken women.

Finding a human to date and then mate was a long shot, but I didn't think my options would be so dismal. It didn't help that I couldn't leave Garnet River very often, if at all.

Camden Miller was still at large, the son of a bitch who had murdered my family ten years ago and tried to take over the clan while I was growing into my leadership role. And I planned to kill him. The coward didn't show his face. He was out there somewhere, plotting to get rid of me. I couldn't leave the clan vulnerable to him, and I couldn't risk giving him easy access to those who wished to aid him.

So I was stuck in Garnet River, like I had been my entire life. Since I was a kid and had been told my parents were found in a nasty car accident and subsequent car fire. I was too precious to the clan. The only surviving Garnet. Because Camden and his family—may they rot in hell—thought they could do better.

Being greedy and selfish was not better. Camden had stolen my family. He was not robbing me of my clan. I'd sacrificed so much for them.

Yet, I feared I wasn't enough for my people. Selma, my guardian, the female who raised me after my parents were killed, was on the city council. They didn't run the town, but the four shifters elected were the ruler's checks and balances. And Selma was retiring soon. She'd been my strongest supporter. The others had been hard but fair, challenging me about subjects I wouldn't have guessed would be an issue. Like a noise ordinance for a small town with little budget for large machinery.

When Selma retired, I needed an ally in a leadership position. Logically, I needed a powerful mate at my side, and the dating app guy who claimed I'd love how his erection curved to the left wasn't it. That had been picture number two.

Selma knocked lightly. I was in my makeshift office. The city council meeting room was an old dining room of a saloon, and this used to be the manager's office. It needed work.

Every building in town needed work.

"Any luck?" she asked quietly.

No one else in the clan knew what I was doing. Just Selma. She didn't like the idea. She preferred the Silver brothers' idea. An arranged mating. With Ronan Jade. The youngest of three kids in the Jade clan ruling family. On paper, it looked like an excellent match.

In reality, Ronan was an arrogant prick.

In reality, his dick pic was probably a lot more impressive than what I had received.

Deacon Silver, the ruler of all the clans as the Silver ruler, thought it was a good idea to have Ronan stay in Garnet River to "see how things turned out."

Ronan had been here for six months. He'd moved into the run-down house next to mine. I didn't know what he thought about possibly mating me. He wasn't exactly trying to get to know me.

"No. No luck." I shut my screen off and scrubbed my face. "Maybe since Ronan's here, I should make a few trips to Minneapolis."

He was cocky, but he wanted Camden dead as much as I did. Camden and his family had nearly killed his sister. Venus lived, but Camden's family died and he was on the run. But in Ronan's months here, he'd concentrated on remodeling the house on the corner and the businesses on Main Street. He didn't give off a sense of being power hungry. The sense of peace in town hadn't been just because the subliminal influence of the Millers was gone. Ronan was trusted by the Silvers. Ronan oozed a sense of confidence and *don't fuck with me* that Garnet River respected. They wouldn't cross him if I was gone for a night.

Selma chewed over my announcement. "It'll take more than a few trips to get to know a human well enough to trust them."

Telling a human guy I was a dragon shifter wouldn't be easy. It was one of the biggest risks a shifter could take. Telling a human other than our mate was forbidden, yet it was hard to mate a human if they didn't know what we were.

The independent girl inside me raged. I didn't need a mate. At least until I was thirty-five and it was mandatory to preserve my sanity. But I was only twenty-three.

Ronan was thirty-three.

He didn't look over thirty. He was in good shape, tall, and stocky. Muscular all over. *All* over. He was—

Ronan was hot. And he knew it. All the single females in town had practically gone into heat when he arrived—and dragon shifters didn't go into heat. We weren't mountain lion shifters.

When I didn't elaborate on my impromptu plan, Selma pressed. "Are you going to tell him you have business or plans in the city or something?"

What if he knew I was lying? I was the ruler, I should come out and tell him I was going to a club. Grab my lady balls and tell Ronan that just because he came to stay in Garnet River to see if we were a good match, I was out looking for a different person.

And if anyone knew what an uphill battle I would be fighting, they'd laugh.

"You're wavering." Selma knew me too well.

"I'm not. It's none of his business."

"You were more confident when you announced you should mate Penn Silver."

I shuddered. Not my best memory. I had thought the same as Deacon. A strong mating, but I'd been relieved when Penn turned me down flat. His heart had been stolen by a Venus. At the time, more like tossed away. I'd rather be friends with Venus and Penn than anything more.

Deacon had wielded the same idea against me and sent Ronan. "That was before we dealt with the Millers. When Camden Miller thought he could claim me."

Her downturned lips said she disagreed. "And if Ronan leaves?"

I almost shouted no. If he left, who would help me with the renovations? Who'd spike my adrenaline with a sexy smirk as he asked me if I wanted to deal with some dick today. Each time he meant the contractors. And each time irritated me more that he didn't mean me.

He hadn't outright rejected me, but he also hadn't left. "It's not like we're hooking up as it is."

She stepped in and closed the door. After what we'd just talked about, I couldn't imagine what she was worried about anyone overhearing. "Has he been sleeping with other females?"

Every morning I expected to walk out my front door and see a female I knew doing the walk of no-shame away from that house.

And every morning, his front door stayed closed. Each day, I expected to hear gossip at the diner. None. Cries of ecstasy from indoors? Nope.

Ronan didn't seem like a guy who could keep it in his pants. His attitude screamed that he thought he was nature's gift to dragon shifter females. Instead, he was a conundrum who pissed me off with his obnoxious advice on load-bearing walls and how shiplap was overrated.

"I don't know if he's been with anyone since he's been in Garnet River." The only scent I got from him was dust and freshly cut wood over his pine-covered-hearth scent.

Selma perched on the chair across from the desk. Her silver hair was pulled back into a twist and despite the dismal local economy, she always dressed in slacks and solid color blouses. "Perhaps... you should try dating him."

"Selma," I hissed.

"It's what he's here for, and I think you may be blocking yourself from an opportunity out of sheer stubbornness."

"It's not as if he's acted interested." So maybe I'd been a tiny bit excited when he'd arrived. Full of consternation, yes, but... Ronan was a snack. Then he'd opened his mouth.

"Make the first move." When my eyes widened, she patted her hair. "Female shifters aren't exactly demure. I haven't been able to teach you a lot about being a leader. I've only served on the council. But it's up to you to get what you need."

She rose and left, leaving the door hanging open.

I stared at the wood grain of the old desktop. My sister had been the oldest. This role would've been hers. But I was here. Selma had done her best, but she didn't possess generations of ruling knowledge.

Ronan did. His parents had been fearsome. Ruthless and aggressive for no good reason. I had worried he would be like them, but he hadn't shown those traits. Perhaps he was good at hiding them.

Perhaps that was why I was nervous around him. Selma and the other three members of the council had tried to prepare me for other rulers like Jade. Silver watched over all the clans, and Deacon Silver had a good reputation, as had his parents. Peridot was a couple hours even farther north of Garnet River. Minnesota had a lot of woods. Large stretches of land for shifters to hide in.

Emerald and Opal kept to themselves.

Letting out a sigh, I looked at my phone and the dismal matches on the dating app.

It'd been six months since Ronan had been here, and we weren't any closer to knowing whether we were a good fit off paper. The pendulum was swinging toward not.

Would Deacon Silver order us to mate? Should I make the first move before that happened?

And if he did, then what? Ronan was older. He might not be a world traveler, but he had more life experience. He'd at least left Jade Hills. With ten years on me, he'd done a lot more than I had. He had all the power. I put a lot of trust in him just by letting him stay. And everyone watched as he worked with me. But he didn't hit on me.

If I had to beg him to mate me too?

The prospect of leaving Garnet River was equal parts exhilarating and terrifying. But I had to do it for me. I had to show the clan I was confident in my power. Begging Ronan to be with me wouldn't accomplish that. I needed to find a male who was actually interested in me.

RONAN

LUST POUNDED THROUGH MY VEINS. The image of only one female branded the back of my eyelids and I damn well kept my eyes shut while I jacked off in the shower.

Tepid water pounded onto my face, but I ignored the temperature. I didn't have much use for a decent water heater when I needed two or more cold showers every day.

Her defiant gaze taunted me. Her cinnamon vanilla smell. Would she moan low and long or do a moan and pant? Could I get her to do both?

My roar echoed off the walls as lightning raced from my balls straight out my shaft. I arched backward, the water hitting my chest and washing my release down the drain as if it never happened. Until next time.

Once my climax passed, I flipped the knob to shut the water off and braced my hand on the wall. My sides heaved while I stared at the rest of the water circling down the drain.

Fuck.

I was going to get calluses on my palm if I kept this up.

A knock broke through my haze. I blinked droplets of water from my eyes and stepped out of the shower.

More knocking. "Just wait!" I bellowed. What the hell was wrong now?

Since I'd taken over as the downtown renovation project manager, Garnet River residents banged on my door with bullshit excuses to disrupt my day. Half the guys wanted a sly way to get me to deal with their issues instead of going to Brighton Garnet, the ruler.

Brighton.

It did no good to think about her. I stepped into my jeans and stuffed my dick behind the zipper before stomping out of the bathroom. I ripped the door open.

My erection that had been waning almost roared back. The defiant reddish-brown gaze that haunted me every time I closed my eyes stared back at me, only the touch of fear was there. The simmering anxiety never left her gaze when she faced me.

And that was why I'd been here six months, jacking off in the shower.

I'd seen the way people had looked at my parents. The underlying terror. The way they feared how my parents could destroy their lives on a whim, which they had so often been known to do.

"What's up?" The question came out as a growl.

Her gaze stuck on my bare chest for several moments before she tensed and lifted her chin. Something about me put her on edge. I didn't know what put the fear there, but she hadn't been able to trust many shifters in her clan. Why would she trust a Jade of all people?

"Can I come in?"

Fuck no. Then her cinnamon vanilla scent would linger in the air and I'd have to take another shower. My water bill was exorbitantly high, and I shouldn't need to cash in a gem from my hoard to pay for it.

I stepped back and let her in, inhaling deeply but quietly to keep from feeling like the old man perv next to her. "Something wrong?"

"Look, we both know why you're here." She ran her hand over the long black braid over her shoulder. She opened her mouth to continue and snapped it shut, blinking as she looked around the room.

Pride threatened to puff out my chest. I had fixed up my house in Jade Hills. It was even older than this, and while this place had been run-down as fuck when I moved in, I had good experience under my belt.

I'd made a cutout in the wall between the living room and kitchen and turned it into an island. During the days, I worked with the contractors downtown, and at night, I sanded and stained trim or removed wallpaper and painted.

Remodeling was my happy place. Fixing up this house kept me sane while living next door to a single female I couldn't put my hands, much less my tongue, on.

"You did all this?" The awe in her voice made my dragon want to show his belly. Dragons didn't fucking do that.

"Is that a surprise, Bright?"

She rolled her gaze to me, irritation ripe in the depths of her irises, but the fear was gone. "Honestly? Yes."

Well, she was honest. "If you didn't think I knew what I was doing, why did you agree to let me take over with the city renovations?"

"Venus vouched for you." She turned to the wall and ran her fingers over my work.

I knew what she'd feel. Smooth paint over a very fine texture. The wallpaper had tested my patience. I had only wanted to shift into my dragon and burn it off eighty or so times when I worked on removing it. But it'd been a treasured distraction from the alluring but young leader of Garnet clan. The beautiful shifter my siblings and the Silvers wanted me to mate.

When Brighton trailed her fingers down the new paint job to the trim tracking four feet above the floor, I felt it in my dick.

"But the detail..." She bent to peer at the trim. The muscles in her legs flexed and my dragon begged to mount her and bite her neck.

That's not how it works, asshole.

"I'm known to be good with my hands, and I pay attention to what really matters." I couldn't help the innuendo in my tone. It usually drove her off faster, giving me a moment of peace where I wasn't degenerating into a rutting beast, but she squared her shoulders.

"I'm going to be leaving for a night."

"Where? Why?" She hadn't been out of Garnet River's boundaries since I'd been here, and from what I'd heard, she hadn't traveled much since her parents died. She was too important to the clan.

The emotions that ran through her expression put me on alert. Subtle glints of panic, wariness, and determination. Add a little defiance, and I was more than intrigued. Why didn't she want to tell me? Irritation flared hot in my chest, but I waited for her to respond.

"I have business."

I braced my feet against the floorboards. My proximity made her nervous. I was surprised she was even in my living room. She'd avoided this house like it was a black hole that could suck her in. "What kind of business, Bright?"

"I need to go to the city for the betterment of the clan, and that's all you need to know. But I'm asking you to keep an eye on things."

She had the council, but she was asking me. Didn't she trust everyone on the council? Or did she trust me more? "When are you leaving? When will you return?"

She lifted her chin. "Tomorrow. The day after."

"Where are you staying?"

There was the panic again. "I don't know—a hotel."

"I'll need to know how to reach you."

"I'll have my phone on me."

"What's the business?"

"Mine. For now." She went around me to the door, her walk stiff, like she was self-conscious.

This female fascinated me. I didn't go after the young females in Jade Hills. I felt too out of touch with their youthful optimism. The way they talked, either too shy or too blatant, and how they laughed at nothing and every-thing. Brighton was as young as them, but the weight of responsibility had robbed her of that laughter.

I'd like to return it, but I ended up pissing her off most of the time.

Before she opened the door, she paused. "Is there an update on the contractors?"

"We're nearing the end of phase one. The diner and the gas station are going strong and everyone's happy." It'd been her insistence to fix up the revenue-producing businesses that would also lift morale. The council members had been split. Selma had supported Brighton naturally. Kiva as well. Wayne had argued for city hall and the post office to go first, but Jimmie had shut him down, insisting the post office and library should be the priority. "We should meet to review phase two."

"When?"

"Now's good."

Her gaze dipped to my bare chest. "Now?"

"Are you busy?" I used the same cocky tone that put her on edge.

She arched a brow. "I have a clan to run."

"And training?"

Her lips set in a line. I'd been bugging her about carrying on the training she'd been doing with my sister, but she'd refused—with me at least. I couldn't be nosy and ask around, or those who Camden had pitted against her would suspect the same as me. She wasn't keeping her skills as sharp as they should be.

"We can review phase two this afternoon before I prepare to leave town." Her tone was firm.

Again, her announcement of leaving Garnet River

gnawed at my patience. What the hell was she doing? "I'll be in your office at two."

"See you then, Jade."

My fingers twitched, like they always did when my clan name left her mouth. I wanted to feel her lips move when she said it.

She walked out the door, and I used the opportunity to watch her ass.

Damn. This girl had me tied in knots, but I refused to make a move on a female who was scared of me.

CHAPTER
TWO

B righton

THE MUSIC BLARED against my sensitive eardrums. I blinked against the onslaught of flashing lights. How could the place be so dark and so bright at the same time?

I gritted my teeth and pressed forward, taking in my surroundings. The first thing I noticed after my vision adapted was that I stuck out.

I wore a red sweater Selma had knitted me two years ago, my black leggings, and my athletic shoes. My dollar store flip-flops weren't a good idea in the winter, but they would've blended in better. I looked like I was ready for a yoga class, not clubbing all night. But I fit in well enough. I'd have to buy clothes in the morning. The frugal part of me refused to splurge just because my family's jewel hoard had been found. I had sold a few of the bigger diamonds to fund the downtown renovations, but I'd have to find ten more hoards of equal value to pay for them all.

Still, it had taken the pressure off. I could update my wardrobe and it'd have the same effect. And I would, but I wasn't buying anything without knowing what style I should go for. From the looks of it, I had a lot of options. My leggings would work, but a less utilitarian top would be needed. A pair of ankle boots or calf-high boots. Or both.

I had kept my hair down, the loose curls flung over my back. I studied the twists and updos of the women dancing and chatting at a nearby table. The hairstyles weren't any different than what the females in my town wore, but I was free to stare—just enough to keep from being creepy. At home, I couldn't risk looking like I didn't know what I was doing. I had to make whatever I did look intentional.

It was exhausting. I wanted to fuck up without worrying that I'd put the town in danger. That my clan would think I was weak.

Weak ricocheted through my brain, summoning Ronan's recurring question. *Have you trained lately?*

I had, but without a partner, it wasn't as effective. Selma met me in the woods for a good sparring session, but it wasn't the same. I wasn't going to throw around an eighty-year-old dragon who was like a mother to me. She could heal, but she was getting older and her healing energy faded each year.

Soon, I'd lose her. Whether it was tomorrow or twenty years from now, it'd be too soon. But it was inevitable. I had learned that lesson early in life.

And then what? Who would get voted into her position on the council? Would I find out that snide Bill

Sonnet was really biding his time until Selma was gone so he could help Camden challenge me and win? Was it Shiloh from the gas station? Wanda from the diner? Boris the café's regular? Were they watching and waiting?

I slid my ass onto an open barstool and openly gawked. The bass reverberated through my bones. It wasn't unpleasant, but the volume would ensure I had a headache in the morning.

I'd have a headache before midnight.

"What can I get you?" The bartender was as handsome as the rest of the guys in the club, though women seemed to be the majority.

Did I catch a hint of shifter?

"Martini—dry." I had no idea what a martini tasted like, but I'd heard the reference enough. Selma loved James Bond, but I refrained from ordering it shaken and not stirred.

"What kind?"

"What?"

He pinned me with a direct stare that was less than impressive. His face said he was a busy guy, I was probably a shit tipper, and he didn't have time for me. "Vodka, cucumber, raspberry, smoky, chocolate, French—what kind?"

"Chocolate?"

He cocked a brow. "Are you sure?"

"No." I clutched my phone like I was going to run. I didn't expect to be this out of my element.

His expression softened, and he leaned across the counter. "Have you been here before?" When I shook my head, he nodded like it was now obvious. "Right. So our chocolate martini has Irish cream and crème de cacao. It's like a dessert."

I liked dessert. "It sounds like a good start."

His mouth ticked up on one side, and he pushed away. I swung around to watch the crowd. This was more of a recon mission. I didn't expect to connect with anyone.

Which meant I'd have to come back. I'd known it, but the realization of how ambitious my plan was astonished me. How was I going to meet a worthy male in this crowd? It wasn't like they wore signs.

It wasn't like I was excited. Driving to the city had been like going for a root canal. I'd never experienced one, but it didn't sound fun.

Did I want to connect so much with someone that I couldn't wait to mate them? Yes. Tendrils of anxiety curled in my stomach. Thankfully, not tonight.

I watched the women who looked closest to my age. They'd go from talking to dancing in the same sentence. They sipped drinks as they laughed. Flipped their hair if it was down. When a song came on that they all seemed to know, several raised their hands and pumped it to the chorus while they belted out the tune. So many selfies. Even more short videos.

If a hot guy sidled up to them, it was immediately clear to me whether they were receptive or not. But not to the guys. Some dudes didn't get the hint, and it didn't matter what species they were.

My gaze skipped to two women making out by a high-top table. Would I ever feel comfortable enough to shove my tongue down someone's throat in public? I'd had to worry about my image for so long, would I be doing it for show, or because I couldn't quit touching the faceless guy from my imagination?

But the guy had a face. That was the issue.

Infuriating green eyes, a deeper green than his sister's. Messy sandy-blond hair like his mind whirred too fast to stop and run a comb through it. He wore worn jeans when he worked, when he ate at the diner, and when he chilled on his back porch with a beer.

It was winter now, but I had missed the best evenings of summer avoiding a chillaxing Ronan.

"Here you go." I turned to find the bartender. He tapped his fingers on the bar top and rattled off a price that made me choke.

How much did this tiny drink cost? He repeated the amount and I handed over more cash than I had planned to spend all night. A chocolate martini was more expensive than the café's lemonade.

It was a one-drink night. Water probably cost at least five bucks for a glass the same size.

I sipped the martini and sweetness with a bite coated my tongue.

A scent wove its way through my nose. A shifter male. Not the one who turned my insides molten before he twisted them in knots. The male approached from behind. I tensed, aware, but pretended I didn't notice.

"Brighton?"

I nearly jumped. The multitude of scents in the room made it seem as if he was farther away. Not right next to me. How did he know me?

I turned to face him and something familiar about the male pulled at my mind. "Yes?"

He wasn't from my clan. A little over six feet tall, he had the top layer of his longish black hair pulled back and tied behind his head. The rest swept the back of his neck. His eyes were a bright green with a yellow tint, almost chartreuse. Peridot. If he had the eye color of his clan, then he was in the ruling family. I clicked through my interaction with Peridot. Memphis was the ruler, and she wasn't even thirty yet, but she had a twin. Maverick was ten minutes younger than her, thus she was the ruler. And Levi. He was a few years older than me.

"Levi." My tone was cautious, my suspicious mind unwilling to be delighted there was another shifter in the place. Yet nothing about me was relieved that there was a single male—of a ruling family, no less. An emotion more like disappointment filled my body. "What are you doing here?"

He shook his head, his expression asking, *What wouldn't I be doing here?* "It's early yet, but my clan—" His gaze flickered to the bartender and the couple next to us he was taking an order from—"my *buddies* like coming here." He leaned in. "A higher ratio of single females to males." His grin was unrepentant.

I had noticed that fact, but his comment surprised me. What were the odds I'd end up at a place shifters frequented? I had hoped to go to a club where I could be incognito, but since I was old enough to eavesdrop, I'd listen to others talk about their lives. So it made sense that I was drawn to a familiar name even if it didn't consciously register. I'd probably heard it casually dropped in conversation. While I'd just as quickly forgotten about it, the place had stood out when I went searching.

I'd walked right into a club where shifters were regulars. Damn.

Why was I upset? It was like a fast pass to a mate. I didn't have to worry about humans and the consequences of spilling our secrets. What were the odds I'd find a human I trusted enough to tell him about shifters in just a few weeks or months?

My rising surliness had to be because it was Peridot. Ronan rubbed me wrong with his arrogance. Peridot had arrogance in spades, especially their gorgeous ruling family.

"So more are coming?" I asked before my silence got more awkward than it was. I took a sip to cover my nerves.

His wink was so quick I almost missed it. "It's your lucky night."

I sputtered over my drink and he laughed, wedging himself between me and the couple next to us. "I guess," I wheezed.

"Seriously, you never go out. What are you doing here?" He wasn't even abashed that he knew I had no social life. He was a sibling of a ruler. It was his job to know all the gossip, so naturally, my business was his business.

I was used to being tracked by my own people, but it added another level of tension—and annoyance—to know the other clans did it. "I'm going out now. Didn't you hear?"

My catty response increased his grin.

For fuck's sake, did I just flirt? A vise closed around my chest. I struggled to keep my panic at bay. I didn't flirt. I didn't. And not with Peridot.

Even though... he was a catch. On paper. It would be prudent to see if this could go beyond a polite conversation. A nice chat would be beneficial. It'd get back to his sister, and she might encourage a mating with a ruling female.

"I'm hearing it now. But I also heard you have Ronan

Jade helping you renovate Garnet River." Knowing resonated in his tone. Had everyone figured out why Ronan was in my hometown?

Had everyone figured out he wasn't interested? "He is." I didn't offer more information.

Levi waited like he was hopeful I would. When I didn't, his eyes crinkled at the corners. His light-brown skin was a few shades darker than mine. His indigenous ancestry wasn't as far back as mine. A couple of my great-great-grandparents had been Métis. One a human woman who'd mated into the clan, and the other a human male. I didn't know Levi's family history. "That bad, huh? What I expected from a Jade."

Defensiveness rose up and refused to be quashed down. "He's fine, actually. I don't have to deal with the contractors. You know how boobs get in the way of that."

His gaze dropped to my chest, and I realized my error. Was that considered flirting? I was so confused.

Interest shone in his eyes, but not any more than I'd expect if I was another young, attractive female.

Did I want to be just another fuck to someone?

Shouldn't that be what I wanted? I was supposed to be after a mate, not random hookups. But I might need the randomness in order to get to the mate.

My martini threatened to crawl up my throat.

"I know all about boobs, Brighton." His grin was practiced.

No, I wasn't special.

But I had to do what was best for my clan and Ronan wasn't offering up more than his carpentry and project management knowledge. "What else do you know about?"

Ugh. It came out flirty, and it was the last thing I felt.

His eyes narrowed and his nostrils flared. I knew what he'd be smelling. A couple hundred perfumes and lotions and colognes. Sweat. More than a few someones had smoked pot. Cigarette and vape odors. But I also knew what he wouldn't smell. My desire.

"You're not into me, are you?" he asked.

"I'm not there." I forced myself to add, "Yet." I had to do something for my clan, but I didn't know Levi that well. Would he see a chance to use a mating bond to usurp me and get his own clan to rule? He was third in line.

He chuckled, a real sound with genuine humor. "Mind if I stick around? I need a break from the game." His dimple flashed with his grin. "Mostly I needed a break from my brother and sister."

"I get it. But hey, if you're going to crash my night, I want you to show me around this place." Hoping I asked in a way that didn't make it sound like I was completely new at the things that seemed to come naturally to our kind, I waited for his answer.

"Yeah, of course." He took my hand. The touch didn't spark against my skin. There was no quiver in my belly. And worst of all, it didn't make me want to preen like the girls I'd been watching get hit on by hot guys all night— the ones who were receptive to the dude.

He led me to the dance floor, leaning close to speak into my ear. There was nothing sexual; the music was so loud. "This is the real mating grounds."

He started pumping his hips, his arms pushing into the air in time with the beat.

Dancing. Right.

I didn't know how to dance. But I'd been pretending

for almost half my life. That made tonight no different than any other night.

~

RONAN

IT WAS MONDAY MORNING, and Brighton hadn't returned to Garnet River until late last night.

What the fuck had she been doing?

She'd parked her little blue Impala right in front of her house and carried her overnight bag inside.

Not that I had been peeking out my living room window once or twice an hour. But I was supposed to keep an eye on the town.

Then she'd stayed gone. All damn night. She didn't call. She didn't check in.

I got out of my cold damn shower and toweled off.

Her absence gnawed at me. I wanted what was best for my people. I would take care of Garnet River no matter what. Our kind needed the help, and my clan had once been in dire straits like Garnet. But without Brighton here over the weekend, my give a shit flagged.

Just as I zipped my pants, there was a solid knock at the door.

That was her.

I knew her knock. How bad did I have it?

I ripped open the door. The cold spray hadn't been enough to wash away my irritation. "About time you showed."

I took a deep inhale, sifting through her vanilla scent

for the hints of another male. I couldn't think of another reason she'd spent the whole weekend in the city.

Nothing but cinnamon vanilla, and my sniff test was a bad idea. The zipper dug into my growing cock.

"Is something wrong?" Confusion lined her brow. "You said you'd have it handled and you didn't call to say otherwise."

I crossed my arms over my bare chest. Her eyes narrowed on mine. She hadn't looked at my chest in the twenty seconds since I'd opened the door. "I don't like being taken for granted."

She tipped her head like she hadn't heard correctly. "Okay... you didn't call and since you're an adult—and Ronan Jade—I figured everything was fine."

"What'd you do?"

"It's personal."

"How personal?"

She scowled. "I came here for an update on the progress."

"You were only gone two days. Over the weekend."

Irritation flashed in her red-brown eyes. Had she done her hair? There was purpose to her curls that was usually missing. She was a wash 'n' go girl. If her hair curled, it curled. If it straightened from neglect, so be it. What the hell was she styling her hair for on a Monday?

"You were complaining about how long I was gone, and now—" She shook her head. "Whatever. The contractors are going to be here in an hour, and I'd like to renovate city hall next."

"I thought you wanted to start on the library." City Hall was the most well-cared-for building on Garnet River's short Main Street.

"I can start on the library, but on the drive, I was

thinking about first impressions and image." She glanced behind her. "Can I come in?"

She usually pushed her way in. Had someone fucked the hostility out of her?

My teeth throbbed. I was at risk of shifting into my dragon in the doorway if I kept posing those questions. I stood aside.

She breezed in, her hair fluttering against my shoulder. A raging erection was on the horizon if she touched me again.

Closing the door, I asked, "What are these mysterious reasons?"

"Oh my—where did you get that cabinet?"

"Hauled it up from the basement. Needs a few touch-ups, but once I wiped all the grit off, I was surprised to see what good shape it was in."

The china cabinet had been heavy as an elephant and the stairwell was as narrow as a slide, but I'd wrestled that beast up the stairs.

She did that thing again. Where she trailed her fingers along the finish as if the piece was talking to her. I'd seen the work she'd done on her house. Between her and Selma, they could've gotten their own TV show. Seeing the life that was still in a structure came naturally to her.

Dragons were energetic beings. Some were more in tune than others. As ruling families, we had to be more adept at tapping into our gifts. But I could watch her stroke wood all day.

Pun absolutely intended.

"Brighton. City Hall? The library?"

She fisted her hand and drew it away. "Image and first impressions are everything with us, and especially with me. I'd rather get the library fit for books and people, but Camden and his supporters might be less likely to mess with me if I look like a strong leader."

"And a strong leader has a strong base to command from." I nodded. "Makes sense. I agree."

She blinked. "You do?"

"Yep."

"I think the council will argue. Not Selma. I've told her my reasoning. But the others…"

"Are going to be harder to convince." A couple of the others rubbed my scales the wrong way. I'd caught Jimmie and Wayne whispering to each other where no one could hear often enough to sap my trust in them.

"They'll accuse me of looking selfish."

"Even though it's your family hoard funding the project and not city reserves." The city didn't have reserves, but several townsfolk forgot that when complaining about Brighton's time line and priorities. Still, an idea was forming.

Brighton could use my help beyond being a project manager. And I wanted her to do something for me. "I think I have a way to make them think it's a fine idea."

Hope entered her eyes, and I grinned like the predator I was. Dragon shifter's days of swooping down on deer and elk were over, but I took my prey in any form. Her gaze turned wary. "What?"

"It'll work, but you and I need to come to an agreement."

Her eyes narrowed. "Which is?"

"I'll start the renovations on the library, and you train with me in the evenings and on the weekends."

"I don't need to—"

I shrugged to negate the deal.

She rolled her eyes. "Fine. I've been practicing with Selma though." She pressed her lips in a line when I gave her the *I know exactly what practicing with Selma is like, and Camden would be much stronger* look.

"Every night. And every weekend."

"I'll be out of town next weekend."

"Then before you go." A bigger male wouldn't infringe on her time. For once, I was small.

"No—"

"Think carefully before you say no, Brighton. I'm here to help ensure the strength of the clan, which means your survival. It's not just fixing plumbing in the downtown diner."

"You had enough spectators." Her tone was catty, and I had to pause for a moment. I'd jumped into the diner when the main sink had flooded the floor thanks to a burst pipe. It'd been during the early stages of renovation and I hadn't wanted the work we'd paid for to go to waste.

It'd been on a frigid day, but I'd gotten soaked wading in there to fix it. I'd taken my shirt and pants off before I left the building and walked home with my wet clothing covering my crotch. Yeah, people had seen. Especially Wanda who'd shown up at my door the next day only to get turned right back around. I had more work to do to save the diner. And I wasn't interested.

Did Brighton think I had a thing with Wanda?

"Jealous?" I purred.

Her eyes sparked as bright as her cheeks. "God, no."

I could smell her lie. She was jealous.

This was... why did it feel so monumental?

This was the confirmation I needed. She didn't *want* to want me, but she did. So my real reason for being here wasn't pointless, and I wasn't some lonely old dude hoping the sweet young thing with firm tits and a round ass wanted to waste her time with me.

My new job was to figure out why she held herself back from me. Was it the age thing? Venus had gotten over her mate Penn's younger age. From the few times I showed up at her place without calling first, I'd heard how much she'd gotten over it. There were some things a brother never needed to hear.

Was it my personality? I couldn't change that. My parents had wanted me to be a brutal, unthinking tool to be used for their purposes. They'd tried to pit me against Lachlan, against Venus, against the town.

No. I wasn't changing for anyone.

"I'll train," she said. "But we're meeting early in the morning on Saturday. I'm... meeting someone."

"Who?"

She gave me a flat stare.

"Your safety—"

"What time in the evenings?"

I wasn't going to get any info. Curiosity burned a hole through my innards, but I'd have to walk around not knowing. Dammit. "Seven." That'd give me twelve hours on the library each day and a couple of hours to spar with her. Maybe I'd come home too tired to jack off. "Starting tonight."

Her cheek twitched. She didn't like taking orders from me, and that was too bad. I enjoyed giving them to her. "We'll meet with the council once we're done with the contractor."

"See you then." I hadn't meant to drop my voice into another deep rumble, but she went stiff and stormed to the door.

"Don't be late, Jade."

"I don't come until it counts."

She made a choking sound as she walked out. My chuckle died in the quiet room.

My plan that had seemed downright brilliant a minute ago sank in. I arranged more time to be around Brighton Garnet. We'd get physical together. Yeah, I'd be tired from the long days, but I'd also string myself tighter than I'd ever been.

But maybe it'd give me a chance to figure out why she avoided the idea of mating me.

THREE

B righton

I ARRIVED at the training spot early. I'd had to cut Jimmie off to do it. He'd been asking who I considered qualified candidates to run for city council. Selma hadn't put in her notice yet. Why was he in a hurry to replace her?

Jimmie was less volatile than Wayne. Kiva practically phoned in her position. But Selma was invested in me and the town. Perhaps Jimmie wanted another Selma and worried they'd get another Kiva.

It was something I should be thinking about. A topic I should've anticipated. I'd told him I was still working through names, hoping he wouldn't call my bluff. My need to get to training early was a handy excuse to shut the conversation down and act like I was on official business.

My training was officially necessary and completely unfortunate.

The chill in the air nipped my skin. Rushing through shedding my clothes, I hissed when my bare feet touched the snow. Once I shifted into my dragon, my skin changing to green scales covered in a garnet hue, the cold was a welcome relief. Shifting didn't hurt. It took energy, and after the first few shifts, there was no disorientation. The crisp smell of snow was in the air and I could hear creatures scratching in their burrows.

This arrangement could be worse. Changing into my dragon on a twenty-two-degree day was better than a ninety-degree blistering heat. The trees could only shade so much.

Reveling in the stretch of my longer bones, I lumbered around the clearing in the trees. Most shifters took to the woods, but this clearing was where Venus and I had been attacked. My clan stayed away from it like it was a bad omen, like Camden was going to make the same move in the same place. I continued to train here like nothing was wrong.

Because nothing was wrong.

I was strong, and I wasn't afraid of an attack from Camden. I'd run him off once, I could do worse given the chance. I would do worse.

I feared the insidious intentions of the male. He was a coward. Greedy and entitled, he thought he deserved this clan because he was a dude and I was an orphaned girl.

"Early?" Ronan's voice broke through the stillness of the winter.

My nostrils flared, more from surprise. How could he sneak up on me like that? I was a damn dragon, yet I hadn't smelled his pine needles covering a warm hearth scent.

It was all that filled my nose now.

He yanked his sweater off. Where I'd worn a jacket over my long-sleeved shirt, jeans, and winter boots with waterproof soles, he'd arrived dressed in just the hoodie, work jeans, and boots he had worked in. A human would be freezing, even after a hike through the woods. But Ronan could melt a puddle of snow in a ten-foot radius from his smoldering appearance.

His bare chest was once again on display. My gaze was weighed with lead when faced with his defined pecs and abs. I struggled to lift my gaze to his face.

I didn't have to. He bent over to tug his boots off, then shed his jeans.

God. I spun around, my spiked tail thumping a tree. His chuckle sent a bone-deep shiver through my body. Energy sizzled in the air when he shifted. It hadn't done that with Venus, but it was difficult not to be aware of Ronan on a different level than I was with his sister.

I turned in time to see a large dragon with forest-green scales covered in a jade-green sheen rushing me. Tempted to dance backward, I lowered my head, aimed low, and met his charge with my own.

It was like bashing a heated wall with my head. I rolled and tried to score his belly with my curled talons. In a real battle, I'd have them out and proud, ready to gouge.

He swayed out of the way and rounded on me. We faced each other, our sides heaving from the quick exertion. His big white teeth were showing like he was grinning. His energy rang with exhilaration. I bared my teeth, excitement surging through my veins.

He lunged again. I chose a different approach for this attack, circling around, put him on the offensive.

He fought like his sister. Not a surprise. But I sensed he was holding back, testing me, seeing where my strengths and weaknesses were. I should be used to it. I shouldn't take it personally. We'd never sparred before. But I tired of being the inexperienced one, struggling to keep up, never seeming to race ahead. Waiting for Camden to attack.

Grappling with Ronan was bringing back memories of the day of the attack. I didn't sense the other male. I knew his smell. There was no sign of him, infuriating me even more.

Ronan slammed his tail into my side, catching me off guard while my thoughts were on the ever-present danger to me and my clan.

I landed on my side. Before I could roll up, Ronan had shifted back to his human shape.

I kept my gaze planted on the underbrush poking out of the snow as I rolled to my feet.

"You were distracted." He stood like he was waiting for me to shift and explain myself.

Dragons didn't have a thing about nudity. We had to be naked to shift without ripping seams and getting caught in hems. Some of the bolder shifters walked through town in the nude between shifts.

I wasn't one of them, but it was due to time. I trained when I could, where I could, and sometimes I got caught up talking to members of my clan. It was easier to be dressed if that happened. But around Ronan, I was resistant to shifting to my nude human form.

"Brighton. You were distracted. I could've gutted you."

I gave him a look that was supposed to say *You could try*, but I ended up averting my eyes. His cock was right there. Hanging like it owned these damn woods. What it'd be like fully—

I made a choking sound in my throat.

"Brighton."

I lifted my gaze, carefully meeting his hard stare.

"You can't let yourself get distracted. If you do it in training, it'll be worse in a real fight where there's more real distractions. Don't let them get you killed."

I bared my teeth this time, but it wasn't for the thrill of the fight. Annoyance burned too close to embarrassment in my chest. A tiny tendril of smoke escaped my nostril.

"I know you know. I'm going to take it up a notch. Ready?"

Dammit. He was taking it easy. My muscles were deliciously sore. More exertion and I'd be stiff until my body healed itself. It'd been too long since I've been pushed.

I needed this.

His energy pulsed in the air again as he shifted. Smooth. Effortless. He was a magnificent creature. I'd grown up hearing how uncouth his clan was, but I'd never believe it by looking at him. His beast was powerful, and he prowled the clearing like a male born into a ruling family.

No distractions. Not Camden. Not Ronan. And definitely not how my belly did a flip and my beast wanted to roll over instead of meeting his charge.

RONAN

. . .

SHE WAS GONE AGAIN.

I swung the sledgehammer into another wall. The built-in bookshelves of the old brick building had been added years after construction, back when wood should've been stronger, thicker, and better quality. But the product had been cheap, and years of the elements getting through broken windows and a leaky roof meant they had to go.

New plans for sturdy bookshelves formed in my mind. I'd build fewer of them, leaving a floor plan that could be modified and adjusted based on the needs of the building. There were several freestanding bookshelves that would be usable given enough TLC.

My thoughts hadn't been on shelving units like they should be.

Why was she so secretive?

I'd given her a lecture on distraction during our first training session. I could repeat those words back to myself, or I'd take myself out with an errant swing.

I dropped the heavy hammer on the floor. The old carpet would have to be ripped out later. I left it on to take the brunt of the demolition. I'd already peeked under it to see what I had to work with. Plywood. No natural hardwood. I'd have to find durable flooring on sale.

Other than that, the building had strong bones and natural character. The maple brown of the trim along the walls and doorways reminded me of the brown hue in a flashing pair of eyes. I was tempted to add a faint red touch to the stain to match Brighton's eyes.

My phone buzzed. I tugged it out, my irritation

making me fumble. I caught it and several missed calls from Lachlan flashed across the screen.

I answered. "Yeah?"

"What's going on?" The urgency in his voice wasn't a casual *Hey, what's up?*

"I'm working. What else would be going on?"

"I dunno, like maybe the female you're there to convince to mate you being out with Levi Peridot."

My hand clenched around the phone. I forced myself to relax before I crushed the device. "What the fuck?"

"You don't know?"

If I was shifted, smoke would be billowing out of my nostrils. "I've been working my ass off to better the foundation of Garnet River and train Brighton. But she's been making a few trips to the city that she won't talk to me about."

"Is she cheating on you?"

I'd discussed some of my progress with Lachlan, and maybe I'd made it sound like Brighton was willing to talk about mating instead of avoiding the topic. He naturally assumed things had progressed.

"We haven't—We're not—"

"Ronan. When you say you're working, is that *all* you're doing?"

I stuffed the toe of my work boot into the gritty carpet. A half-moon of dust formed from my demolition progress for today. "It's slower going than I thought."

"Must be if she's out with someone else. A Peridot, Ronan?"

"What about fucking Levi Peridot?" I didn't have much to do with them. The sister was the ruler. There was her twin, and then Levi. I knew little about them other than they thought they shit gold nuggets. Most clans had an ego. Jade's had been dangerously narcissistic until my parents died in a house fire. Lachlan was turning that around. The Peridot kids had been born when their parents were older, more indulgent. They were spoiled, basically.

"His brother called asking why Levi's entertaining Brighton in Minneapolis when she's supposed to be with you. Memphis doesn't want a beef with us. So why's she with him?"

Good damn question. "Maybe they're friends or something."

"Friends that go to clubs shifters are known to frequent to find partners they don't have to keep secrets from?"

Fuck. "What club?"

"Goddammit, Ronan. The Silvers were confident you could win her over."

They were the only ones. "She's scared of me."

"What? Why?"

"I don't know. I haven't been able to figure it out, but I finally got her to train with me. Still, she holds herself back."

"Ronan." That tone of my brother's made me grind my teeth. It was his lecture tone. Calm and unwavering, the opposite of our parents. "You need to figure it out before that Peridot dick puts a ring on it. Otherwise, you're going to come back here, talk shit at me all day in my office, and then settle for some female you're not happy with."

"How do you know I'd be happy with Brighton?" Or that she'd be happy with me.

"You're there, aren't you? We both know you would've found a way out of complying with Deacon's orders. And you wouldn't be taking your sweet damn time if you didn't think she was worth it. You'd have tested the waters and got the fuck out if you didn't want her."

I hated that he knew me so well. But relief sifted through me just the same. I was on the right track, but I needed to move faster.

Only she was out of town, and she'd asked me to watch over things.

I ran through my options. Making my decision, I said, "What's the club's name?"

FOUR

B righton

The music was just as loud as last time, but the assault against my ears was no longer new. I adapted quicker, tuning out as much as I could.

I chose a different spot at the bar. Routine wasn't a single female in the city's best friend. I had done my research. I was a dragon shifter but being overly confident could get me into trouble too. Hard to explain how I tossed a full-grown man a hundred yards, so I had to avoid the experience. And this time, I was ready with a drink order.

"Strawberry Truly." Several humans were drinking cans with the name. I'd blend in and try something different, hopefully less sweet and tempting than the chocolate martini. I liked strawberry; might as well start there.

An arm draped over my shoulders just as I cracked open the can. Levi's fir balsam and amber scent surrounded me. After a week of training in Ronan's pine-covered-hearth smell, I nearly shoved Levi away.

"Ready for more enlightening?" he asked.

Without saying his suspicions out loud, Levi had run me through dancing, ordering drinks, mingling, and what to watch for shifters in the city. I'd soaked up all the information without gushing about how I needed every scrap he gave me.

"I'm here, aren't I?"

He grinned and held out his hand. "Then let's find a booth."

Dread pooled in my gut. A booth? I'd seen what went on in booths. I didn't come here ready to crawl onto Levi's lap while I sucked his face off, then moved farther south...

He laughed. "Your face! Don't worry. It's for observation. But you should get used to touching a guy without flinching or looking like you'd rather vomit and lick it up like a wolf shifter."

I nudged him. "Don't get me in trouble with wolf shifters." I had enough problems with my kind of shifter.

"Then come on. I promise whatever I do will just be for show and you can set all the limits you want."

He clasped my hand and pulled me behind him. "I'm not afraid of touching you."

He glanced over his shoulder and cocked a brow. "Sure thing, Garnet."

I wasn't afraid. But my stomach knotted when his hands were on me. "Why are you doing this for me anyway?" Did he have ulterior motives? Was his sister planning to challenge me and take over the clan?

He turned to face me. "I know what you're thinking—

I must have something to gain. The truth is that I'm bored. You're a ruler, so I can trust you're not kissing up to me because of Memphis and Maverick. Well, you might be, but you're on the same level."

I nodded. "I'd like to be on good terms with your family, but it's not critical."

"Exactly. You're also the one in charge. Memphis has her hands full. As her second, Maverick is also busy." He shrugged. "I'm not as necessary. I'm young, but I've been coming to the city for years. It gets old."

He didn't have a place or a purpose. I had more to gain from his friendship than he had from me. "Okay."

We crossed close to the dance floor and he turned, swaying his hips. I let the bass beat through me, matching his movements. Just like training for a fight, the dance moves were coming easier. If I wasn't so tired from battling the way my dragon wanted to submit to Ronan while we fought, I'd blast music in my house and cut loose. No one was there to see me. It would be freeing. But training with Ronan drained me, mentally and physically.

Levi grabbed my hand again and tugged me closer. I matched his movement, growing more comfortable with his touch. Not enough to crave it, but enough to think this endeavor could help me get over wanting a male who didn't seem interested.

And if he was? That would be worse. The longer I was around him, I knew it. He was powerful, confident, and knowledgeable. I didn't have much else to lose, but I couldn't lose it to him.

Levi spun and danced us toward the booth. "Slide on in, Garnet. I'll make sure you're really comfortable."

A wall of heat slammed behind me. "What the hell is going on?"

Ronan.

I spun around. Shock and elation crashed together inside my chest. My heart raced. He was here.

Wait. He was here? "What are you doing? Who's—"

He pushed me into a booth and scooted in next to me. Levi's smirk refused to fade as he slid around the half-circle seat.

"Ronan—"

"You two?" He wagged a finger between us. "You've been sneaking around to hook up with a Peridot?"

Levi's humor faded. "You make it sound like a bad thing, Jade. Jealous?"

Ronan gave him a look that should've withered his balls, but Levi wasn't fazed. Ronan's sharp green gaze switched to burn into me. "Brighton?"

"I don't have to justify my actions to you." I was close to sounding like a petulant child.

His glare touched on Peridot, then me again. "Wanna do this here?"

Levi held his hands like he was surrounded by an opposing army. "We were having fun together." He leaned forward when hostility poured off Ronan. "With our clothes on." Reclining, he spread his arms across the back of the booth.

Two males from ruling families were having a power struggle and I was in the middle.

I ranked above both of them. Levi had done nothing to incite Ronan's wrath. Ronan felt like I lied to him. He thought I was using him.

His feelings were justified. He wasn't getting paid for

his work. If nothing, he'd spent his own money along with his time.

I was being inconsiderate. "Levi, would you mind giving me a few minutes with Ronan?"

Levi gave me a quick wink. "You're gonna cut me loose, even for a few minutes? I might get snatched up."

Chuckling, I said, "Go ahead. I don't want to leave anyone disappointed."

He slid out the other side, his grin in place, and aimed it at an irritated Ronan. His words were directed to me. "You have my number if you need it."

"She won't," Ronan growled.

I swatted his abdomen. God, it was rock hard. "Quit acting like a caveman."

"Our kind predates cavemen."

I rolled my eyes. "Who's watching over the clan?"

"If the clan can't tolerate both of us being gone for five hours—"

"Ronan." I let all my annoyance show in my tone. I knew the details, dammit.

"Selma. She's in my house, moving around, keeping the lights on like I'm there."

Smart move. It wouldn't work forever, but if he planned to come here and turn back, then it would be enough.

"Care to tell me why you're here trying to get laid when we both know why I'm in Garnet River?"

Direct. He'd finally addressed the unspoken topic between us.

I chewed the insides of my cheeks. He'd been helping me. I refused to lie to him, but the truth wasn't easy either.

"Brighton." He sighed and all the hostility from

earlier drained out. "If you don't want to mate me, all you have to do is say so. I'll still stick around and help with the contractors. I'm not like my parents." His jaw tightened. "I don't expect favors. I refuse to use or bully someone into—"

I wrapped my hand around the back of his neck and pressed my mouth to his. He jerked like my lips pumped several volts of electricity into him. Then he froze.

I pulled back and licked his taste off my lips. He'd had steak and strawberry-flavored mineral water. The kind I liked.

Why had I done that? I had no business knowing how good he tasted. How nice his lips felt under mine. I had to stay strong.

He stared at me, his expression mixed with confusion and disbelief.

Awkwardness settled between us like a weighted blanket.

I licked my lower lip. "I'm sorry. I—"

He yanked me to him, practically on his lap if it wasn't for the tabletop, and claimed my mouth. He dominated the kiss from the instant our lips touched. His tongue swept inside and I fumbled. I cupped his face and backed off without breaking contact, slowing the sensory assault that was Ronan's mouth on mine.

He carefully broke away, his gaze hooded, his eyes dark. "Shit. I'm sorry."

"No." I didn't move away from him. I was twisted and pressed against him. His leg was under me, but I wasn't quite on his lap. "I... ugh. It's just that..."

I deliberately pushed back, putting a foot of space between us. Far enough away that I couldn't easily clamber on top of him, but close enough that we could talk quietly and our words would be eaten by the music. "It's not that I'm not interested. I am but…"

Did I really have to spill all my secrets to the male sitting as still as a statue ready to listen to me?

The male who'd tracked me down in a big city to find out what the hell I was up to. The male who sort of admitted he hadn't been hitting on me because I had seemed uninterested.

"You're in your thirties," I said. "You've had life experiences."

His brows dropped. "Jade Hills is in rural North Dakota. It's like Garnet River, and I'm not exactly well traveled."

I pinched the bridge of my nose. "I know, but you've done stuff. You've been with…people."

"Have I fucked around? Yes. You want to fuck around?"

Frustrated, I blew out a gusty breath. "I haven't fucked at all."

He was back to being stone still, but probably from shock this time. "Excuse me?"

I let out a derisive snort. I didn't want to be ashamed, but wasn't that why I was here? Embarrassment? "That was my first kiss. Believe it or not." I winced. "It's probably easy to believe."

He scowled as if he didn't approve of my disparaging comment. "So you're here to what?"

"To not feel like such a—to feel more—" I faced forward. It was easier to admit this part without looking at him. "The last ten years of my life, I've had to prove myself. I've had to watch my back. I didn't know who to trust. It seemed like everyone had some kind of advantage. Some sort of power over me. Size. Money. Popularity."

"You don't want that with your mate?"

"I *have* to mate. There's already a power discrepancy there because so far my choice is you. Hell, maybe Levi would be willing."

A low growl emanated from him.

When I looked at him, it cut off. "I don't need another power dynamic to fight against."

"So you want to fuck around?"

No. "I want experience."

"That's why you're coming here?"

I nodded. "I think Levi senses that I'm sheltered. He's been mentoring me. But we haven't done anything. I'm not interested."

"Who are you interested in?"

"It's not a who," I said on a sigh, hating the hurt I was sensing from him. There was a male I was too interested in, but I'd give him part of the truth. "Just life. When I first came here, I annoyed the shit out of the bartender because I didn't know how to order a drink."

He thought about that for a moment. "It's not always about what we've done. Most of us aren't different than you, Brighton. We fake it 'til we make it."

"But most shifters have hit the city before they're twenty. Most shifters have"—I lowered my voice—"kissed a guy before they're well past the legal age to vote, drink, and smoke. We have to mate by the time we're thirty-five. Most shifters don't take their time with this."

His demeanor softened. "But you couldn't trust anyone to get close to you."

"No one wanted to. Camden scared them away with

his bullshit claims on me." I'd been off-limits to my town since my family died. And Ronan felt just as off-limits since I was afraid I'd turn everything over into his capable hands if he demanded it.

~

RONAN

CAMDEN SCARED *them away with his bullshit claims on me.*

I was no different than Camden. I had driven Levi away, at least from the booth, but I would've done more. The hell he wasn't interested. He might've wanted little more than friendship, but he'd love a friends-with-benefits situation. I could smell it on him.

He was on the dance floor with his tongue buried down some woman's throat. Another girl was a better place for his tongue than Brighton.

My presence in Garnet River was keeping her from making any meaningful connections with males her age without Camden's shadow.

I wasn't my parents. I wasn't going to bang into someone's life and warp it to meet my own. Yes, she needed a mate. But she was inexperienced.

"I'll help you."

She blinked. "Excuse me?"

"You want to dance, we'll dance." I didn't fucking dance. When I walked into the place and saw her hips circling close to Levi's, I nearly stripped down and let my dragon out. It'd be easier to rip him apart.

"You dance?"

I shook my head. "Doesn't matter. How 'bout you go

out there? I'll watch over you."

She didn't move. "What about Garnet River?"

Shit. I couldn't stay overnight with her. "I've got an hour. I can push it to two. Go do your thing. Explore."

The word was sour on my tongue. I wanted to lay her open on the table and claim her.

I was not like my parents.

I had to remind myself of that a lot around her.

"But... what if a guy approaches?"

I could've ground my teeth to dust, but I said, "Do your thing."

"You don't mind?"

Fuck, yes. I minded. "I can control myself. Despite what people think of Jades."

"I don't think that," she said quietly.

"Because my sister changed your mind." I tipped my head toward where Levi was grinding against the woman whose tonsils he claimed. "He does. His siblings probably do. But I can control myself."

"Oh. Okay." She pointedly looked past me. If I didn't move, she'd have to scoot all the way around the booth.

I got out and stood aside for her. "New clothes?"

I knew they were new. From the blood-red pants to the cream off-the-shoulder sweater to the black suede boots. She was sexy as hell, but she also looked like she demanded to be taken seriously. Some might accuse her fashion of being too mature, but that was her. Forced to adult since she'd been a teenager.

"I tried to fit in better, but I think I'm still off."

"You look good."

"But you're old." Before I could die slowly inside, she snickered and sashayed toward the dance floor.

Her behavior made it harder to keep my hands off her.

She wanted to live a little. She wanted experience. Not from me.

I got the message loud and clear.

I rubbed my hand across my face, but really I wanted to stamp in the feel of her against my lips. The taste of her seltzer drink stayed on my tongue. It was sweet like her. Crisp, with a touch of innocence.

She closed her eyes and swayed to the beat of the music. My pulse throbbed in time with the bass, forcing me to sit or show the club the bulge in front of my pants.

Girls danced around her. Some in pairs, many single. A few guys had noticed the throng of solitary women. They started moving closer. Clumsy predators hunting their prey.

I was so intent on watching their advance, I didn't notice Levi until his shadow fell over me. "Why aren't you out there with her?"

Telling him to fuck off seemed a bit much, so I said, "Because." When he sat on the other side of the booth, I pried my gaze off Brighton. "Why aren't you balls deep in that human?"

"She wants a toy to bring home to daddy. Those get too messy for my taste, and I'm not talking about bodily fluids."

The human was indeed stalking another single guy, similar in age and dress as Levi. I looked down at my work jeans and boots. My hoodie was dotted with white spackle.

I didn't fit in. My age was in line with everyone else here, but I doubted many folks in this crowd earned their living outside of an office. Their idea of getting their hands dirty was a quick flip of a house done by cheap contractors with no consideration for the bones and character of a structure. Maybe on their weekends, they'd find an old vanity to dress up with chalk paint or whatever was hot on HGTV.

This crowd didn't make a living getting their hands dirty. They took care of the investment portfolios, retirement options, and assets of those who did. My crowd was on the outer edges of downtown, in bars with dust on the window ledges. In those places, the neon lights were thanks to the booze and liquor signs on the walls.

I sucked my lips against my teeth. Some dude was creeping up on Brighton.

"Shit might get messy here," Levi murmured under his breath.

I shot him a glare. I wasn't a part of this crowd, but other than his clothes, he wasn't either. "What are you doing here?"

"Having fun."

I kept my stare steady on him. Better than charging the dance floor and ripping the still beating heart out of the chest of the asshole grinding on Brighton. "Think any of the women here would fit into Peridot Falls?"

"I'm a little young to settle down, but our kind hangs out here too. It's not like there's anything going on at home." Bitterness dripped from his words.

"Isn't that a good thing?"

"The walls are closing in, Ronan. Thanks to all the upgrades in technology, we get to witness the big wide world out there. Yet we're each tied to our clan. It's not like fresh meat moves to tiny clan towns."

"What's your sister going to do?" I didn't have to specify. I knew he was talking about mates.

"Are you offering?"

The corner of my mouth curled up. "No."

"Brighton, huh? I thought so." He reclined in his seat. A server dropped by and he ordered some bougie drink I hadn't heard of. I stayed away from the stuff. It was hard to get a shifter wasted, but not impossible. Drinking faster than healing could happen, and voilà—intoxication. Keep drinking and it'd drown out good sense.

That was how my dad had done it. And when he was drunk, Lachlan and I paid the price. I had a beer once in a while. This wasn't the place to lower my inhibitions, or the man with his sights on Brighton would suffer.

"She's young." I worked my jaw. That bastard had better not touch her.

Brighton's back was to me, but she'd been pivoting to keep Grinder from humping her ass.

"She's not that young."

I grunted, my eyes narrowing. Brighton was like a top out there, trying to keep the perv from accosting her. I was halfway out of the booth when she spun on the man, shoved a finger in his face, and growled at him as she told him to leave her the fuck alone.

I didn't know it was possible to growl and talk at the same time.

Levi chuckled. "Nice."

I eased my ass back on the seat, but didn't take my attention off her. "He's not going to leave her alone."

"Nope." He could've sounded less gleeful. "She wanted the human woman experience, she's going to get it."

"Is that what she said?" She'd talked to him before me?

"Nah, man. It's obvious. A lot of our females come here for the human girl experience. The fancy drinks. The carefree atmosphere. To find out if reality TV is actually reality."

"Is that why you're here?" The curiosity kept me rooted. Brighton continued dancing, but her shoulders were tense and she was giving Grinder the side-eye. His expression was now brooding, with a hint of resentment.

"It's why I first came. I stay for the entertainment." His grin spread. "And it's on."

The grinder swept close to Brighton, his pelvis thrust out, his hands at the ready for an ass grabbing. Millimeters away from touching her, she rounded on him. Maintaining eye contact, she twined her fingers through his and twisted his wrists out until he was immobilized.

People around her could probably hear her over the music. I listened hard, barely catching her words, but I paired what I heard with the movements of her lips.

"If you lay one finger on me, I'll twist your hands off." She jerked her grip and he winced, letting out a yelp. "If that thing in your pants even brushes against me, I'm going to twist that off too and stir my martini with it."

A burly man wove through the crowd.

Levi rose. "Shit, the bouncer. He's pro asshole."

"L-let go!" Grinder shouted.

She released him, giving him a push as she did. He stumbled back. The bouncer plowed through the dance floor and reached the clearing that had formed around her.

He jerked his thumb toward the door. Fire laced Brighton's eyes and she softened her knees like she was taking a fighting stance.

"That's my cue." I rushed to the floor, shouldering the onlookers.

"Why do I have to leave?" Her indignant shout resonated over the music. "He's the pervert!"

"I haven't touched you!" the guy cried, and he gave the bouncer a *you know how these women are* look.

"Both of you. Leave." At least the bouncer wasn't letting Grinder continue his stalking.

"Brighton."

She spared me a glance but spoke to the bouncer. "He was trying to grope me."

"Whatever." The bouncer tipped his head toward the exit. "Go. Both of you."

A dark brow ticked up. "So you'd kick us both out together where he could take his anger out on me?"

The bouncer stabbed a beefy finger into his chest. "My concern is inside this building. I said leave. Or do I have to call the cops?"

Grinder's smirk turned smug. "Ladies first." I shouldered past him, sending him reeling. "What the hell!"

I wrapped an arm around Brighton and sized up the bouncer. "I'll do your fucking job and make sure she gets to her car without interference."

"You two?" His enraged expression must mean I hit a nerve. That big finger waggled between us. "Don't ever come back. You're fucking done here. Out."

Brighton's body went rigid like she was going to argue his decision. I nudged her to get moving. In her ear, I said, "There's plenty of other places to go. You don't need the trouble."

She softened against me, and damn, I could get used to her curves. Our training sessions had been nothing but torture. I got physical exercise, but my self-control was the buffest thing on the planet.

Brighton

"It's bullshit." I fought the urge to return to the club and knee the dick bouncer in the junk. He only liked flexing his power. He didn't care about the people he was there to protect.

Ronan continued to drag me after him. "His attitude is bullshit, but he's doing the job the club wants him to do. They only want to protect their business. The people are replaceable as far as they're concerned."

I jerked my arm out of his grip and instantly regretted it. We'd touched before but not sustained contact. The sizzle that was missing from Levi's touch was definitely there with Ronan. The palm of my hand was warm and I wanted to cradle it to my chest. "It would look bad for the club if a girl got accosted in their parking lot."

"And I'm sure our kind has been saving their ass."

I stopped. "You think males are walking women to their cars?"

Ronan turned to face me. The streetlights cast shadows over his face, making him look like a sinister Jade. A shifter from the clan we'd all heard about while growing up. Even as a ruler, I should be cautious, but Ronan had acted like he was single-handedly changing the reputation of his clan. I would believe it if I wasn't friends with his sister.

"This place is a meat market," he said. "But it's also potential. We're on a time line and our clans are isolated. Options are wide open for humans. They have apps and clubs, but there's little stigma facing those who choose to stay single their whole lives instead of marrying an asshole who sticks around. Finding mates has always been hard for shifters, but we've always been able to find humans willing to tolerate our society in order to get family or society off their back. But we can't. And saving humans—women—makes us the instant hero. Their defenses drop faster."

"Sounds like you've used the same tactic."

"I thought about it, but I don't want to start a relationship with a lie."

"The danger is very real."

"But the intention behind helping them is selfish."

He was a good guy. Even more dangerous to me. He would be good for Garnet River. Would I think he'd be better?

So what had he been planning on doing? I had over a decade before I had to worry about being single. His countdown clock had started. "Do you think we'd be happier?"

"What do you mean?"

"If dragons didn't agree to take the human form. If we still commanded the skies, mated when we wanted to, and gave birth every other century?"

"Do you think our ancestors would've agreed to give up immortality if they were happy?"

I often imagined what it was like then. Brutal. Cruel. But I also wouldn't have had a close-knit family get ripped away as easily as they had. "We had no choice."

"There's always a choice, Bright. Your job to rule in a way your descendants won't regret."

Why did he have to be sexy and insightful? Why did he have to be older and more experienced? The whole package that made up Ronan Jade made me feel inferior, and I'd had enough of that in life. "I'm parked in the corner."

A line formed between his brows. "By the fucking alley?"

I hadn't been able to help myself. I was supposed to play it safe, but I'd been the rebellious kid until I'd been left the only kid. "Better me than a lone girl a douche bouncer kicks out."

"Hey!" The hostile shout came from behind me.

I had to turn to face the threat instead of marinating in Ronan's low growl. When I saw who shouted, my irritation grew. Not only was it the man from the dance floor, but he'd interrupted an enlightening and private conversation with Ronan. There was no one to spy on us in the city.

"What?" I asked. "Couldn't harass me enough inside?"

"Brighton," Ronan said, speaking only loud enough for me to hear. "You're governed by human laws right now."

I'd been governed by so many damn standards over the years. The laws of humans. The ancient rules of my kind. How I was supposed to act. What I was supposed to say.

The bouncer tipped my patience dangerously to the low end.

The man flung his arm toward the club. The only other people outside were on the other side of the street, and I scented no shifters. "You did that on purpose!"

"I got myself kicked out while I was having a good time?"

"You teased me." The guy continued to stomp toward me.

Ronan tried to step between me and him. I flung my arm to the side and flattened my hand against his impressively solid chest. I was tempted to keep it there. "I didn't. You're a creep who doesn't like getting told no. I bet women say it all the time to you. No. No. No. No."

The human's nostrils flared, but he didn't stop.

"No," I said again. He kept coming. Ronan's energy was coalescing next to me, but I'd tear him apart if he tried to deal with this. I'd had it. With everything. "If you don't stop, I'm going to hit you."

"Not if I—"

I punched him. The smack of my skin against his, the crack of bone, and his outraged cry filled the night. He stumbled backward, attempting to catch his balance on the slippery cement, finally falling on his ass. The little bounce was satisfying. He wailed and clutched the left side of his face.

Ronan leaned forward to peer at him. "Thank you for pulling that punch."

"I'm not a fool." I tossed my hair over my shoulder. "Like you said, I'm governed by human laws." I spun away and stalked to my car. Ronan and I needed to get far away from this guy. "I'll cancel my room and drive home tonight."

"No," Ronan said.

I was feet from my ride when I stopped and faced him. "No?"

He shook his head. "You're in town. Go to the room. Enjoy some room service, maybe get a massage in the morning. Live a little. I'll go back to Garnet River and watch over everything until you return."

"What if I go to another club?" I wanted to know this so intently I startled myself.

He shoved his hands into the pockets of his work jeans. What would he look like if he dressed up for a night out? It seemed impossible that he could get sexier. If he dressed like Levi, he'd look like a bull in tap shoes. "Then dance and watch your back. Try to avoid pissing some human douche off."

I swallowed down the dejection. He cared about me but he didn't want me. I forced my attention back to the conversation. "It was his fault."

"I know. And if he were in my clan, there'd have been a reckoning." He glanced over his shoulder where the guy was rolling to his hands and knees, still whimpering.

"He should get to the hospital." I hadn't pulled my punch that much. Lessons weren't learned from a tickle.

"I'm not offering."

"Me either."

He smirked and I grinned. This was the first time I'd been comfortable around Ronan. Not overly self-conscious. Not like a high school girl crushing on a college guy. Not like I was inferior.

For a few minutes we weren't shifters from ruling families tasked with protecting our clans. We were two shifters and nothing more.

"Good night, Ronan. Drive safe."

"Night, Brighton. Sleep tight."

I would. I'd order a pizza, take a bath, and when I went to bed, I'd get myself off while picturing Ronan in his steel-toed boots and worn jeans, staring at me on the dance floor.

FIVE

R onan

I WAS WORKING in the library, blasting what a girl I'd dated once called bro-country. On my knees, I pulled old trim off, wondering if my natural healing ability was strong enough for the repetitive stress on my joints. I hadn't felt like an old fucker until I met Brighton.

I also hadn't felt like a needy partner who had to be updated on their significant other's every move. But here I was, disgruntled once again. Brighton hadn't messaged me at all on Sunday. And it was another Monday I was waiting for word from her. She hadn't called. She hadn't stopped over.

She didn't owe me for driving to Minneapolis and helping her. She hadn't asked. But I thought we crossed a line in our relationship. We weren't an us, but we were more than we were before.

Footsteps sounded behind me. I had heard someone enter, but I waited for them to reveal themselves. It was what determined how I responded.

"Ronan." Jimmie Schrader. From the council.

"Jimmie. How's it going?" I yanked another piece of trim. There was enough in this damn place to keep me busy all week. The town was small, but Brighton's grandparents had believed in the power of reading. Too bad the place hadn't been finished enough to add books. They'd expended their time and money, and times had gotten tough. The Garnets had been on the right track until Brighton's parents had died.

"Good. Yourself?"

"Living the dream." I would be if I could go home to Brighton in my bed.

Jimmie chuckled and wandered through the library with his hands on his hips. He was a slender male in his sixties. His mate had been older and she'd passed. He had two adult children who lived in town. I hadn't been able to get a good read on them. They were congenial to Brighton, but they kept to themselves.

The post office was Jimmie's baby. Wayne wanted it fixed up, but Jimmie was stalling. He was the local postmaster and he controlled the building. I wasn't looking forward to discussing renovations with him. He'd been ornery just letting the contractor in to evaluate structural soundness.

"I'm glad Brighton's decided to revive this old thing."

I had offered, but it benefited Brighton to let him think it was her idea alone. "She has plans."

"Any idea when you're getting to the post office?"

I scooted to the left to tear off another piece of trim. "You'll have to talk to her."

When I glanced up, he'd almost hidden his irritation. "Sure. Just thought I'd do the two birds, one stone thing. Besides, the contractors are ripping off wood paneling in city hall. It's loud."

I could hear them from here. Human construction workers weren't as sensitive to noise as the rest of us. They weren't touching Selma's apartment, but she had refused to temporarily move anyway. "I do what the boss tells me to."

Jimmie's grin was just short of friendly. "Sure you do. In case you see her before I do, let her know I'd like to talk to her."

He'd probably see her before me. I worked for another two hours, the memory of the cream top against her bronzed skin drowning out the strain in my body. I kept the music loud on my Bluetooth speaker and tried to identify the longing in my chest.

When Brighton walked in, I didn't turn right away. I had my pride.

She tapped the music off on my speaker. "How are renovations coming?"

Irritated, and okay, maybe a little hurt, that she chose a workday, at my place of work, to check up on progress, I yanked another piece of trim off. "Good."

I crawled to another section and loosened the end with the claw of my hammer. The trim had too much water damage to use again. That left me open to removing it however brutally I wanted. And after yesterday, I had some aggression to wear off.

After Saturday night, I had more than aggression to deal with. The tiniest brush of my blankets and I was hard. When I shut my eyes, I saw her ass shaking in the club. I tasted her on my lips.

With a growl, I ripped the trim off.

"What's wrong?" she asked.

"Nothing." I kept my back to her and crawled to another section. Was there a wall that needed removing? I needed to sledgehammer something.

Her footsteps crunched dust and debris. She squatted next to me, her cinnamon vanilla scent rolling over me. I shut my eyes and fought the urge to flip her over, strip us both down in the musty reference section of the library, drive into her, and put my mark on her neck.

"Ronan."

I didn't need a hammer to pry the trim loose. I dug my fingertips in and yanked.

She put her hand on my arm. I whipped my head to look at her, and she withdrew her hand, her eyes wide.

"Are you okay?"

Blinking, I forced all my surging emotions down. Imagining a lid slamming shut over them, I nodded. "I'm fine. I just didn't sleep well last night."

"You can take a day off. You've been working nonstop since you got here."

To keep my mind off how I wanted to ravage her. "I'm fine."

"I'm here to help. I can spare a day out of the office."

"Fuck no." I grimaced, thankful my back was to her.

"It's my clan's library." Her voice was flat and the acrid scent of her hurt laced the air.

I sat back on my feet. There went my quiet day to work. "Fine." I pushed to my feet. "Finish ripping the trim out. I'll start measuring and staining the new stuff."

I made the mistake of looking at her. Her jeans were well worn and hugged her curves as closely as I wanted to. She wore an old gray shirt with a frayed hem. The material had thinned, especially around her tits where they brushed against the material. She'd pulled her hair back and braided it. Her fresh face and rested energy amped up my crankiness. I wanted to turn that energy on me. I wanted to devour it.

Her brows pinched together as she studied the space. I had ripped out trim and carpeting in the main browsing area. This was the side room that could be used for other media or meetings, maybe offices. That was one of the things I would get Brighton's opinion on when the demolition was done.

"Are you sure you want to get the new trim ready this early?" Her gaze stroked over the walls covered in old wallpaper that was going to be a bitch to get off. Fucking wallpaper. The walls would need TLC before I could paint them the color we decided on.

We. Why did I like that sound so much?

"I think I know what I'm doing," I half snarled.

"Did you decide on a color scheme?" The hurt was back. I was being unreasonable.

"No." But the new trim boards she'd ordered when it was on sale were in the loading area that subbed as a garage bay. The space was the best ventilated for staining, and even better, it was across the building from where Brighton would be tearing out trim. "But I can do it while you're kicking up dust."

"So? The color?" She stuffed her hands in the back pockets of her jeans, causing her tits to jut against the fabric of her shirt.

I needed to get somewhere private and calm my unpredictable dick down. I hadn't had this little control over my body since my earliest teen years. "Stain is fucking stain."

She held her hands up. "What the hell, Ronan? Is it a case of the Mondays?"

My irritation mingled with sexual frustration, turning into something I didn't want to deal with. Something that only pushing her against the wall, burying my tongue down her throat, and feeling those strong legs wrap around me would solve.

"Yep. That's it." I popped up and stormed to the bathroom.

The first thing I had done in the library was get the sink and a toilet working. I wasn't soft, but using a portable outhouse in below zero temperature wasn't a necessity to prove my masculinity. I didn't have to suffer, or make anyone else suffer, to show everyone how tough I was.

I flipped on the cold water, rinsed my hands and splashed some on my face. If a cold shower could barely dent the unbridled lust charging through my body, this little splash didn't have a raindrop's chance in hell.

The door banged open behind me. "Listen—"

"What the fuck, Bright." I whirled, forgetting about the monster in my pants. "What if I'd been taking a piss?"

"It's not my job to control your stream." She slammed her hands on her hips. "What is your attitude about? This is next level for you. And after this weekend, I thought things were different."

I crowded her toward the wall. She didn't stand her ground. She let me, and fuck if that didn't make my dick even harder. "You thought? You know what I thought? That you'd come back and talk to me? That you'd treat me like I was more than some meathead swinging a hammer?" I stopped, barely touching her.

She frowned, taking a deep breath that made the tips of her boobs graze my chest. "You're mad at me?"

"Yeah, I'm fucking mad. I said I'd mentor you, help you get life experiences." More of the truth was in danger of slipping out than I wanted. "But don't treat me like a fucking tool. I'm not here for you to use."

She could use me any way she wanted. But I'd also wanted to please my parents at one time. And they'd used me.

"Okay?" Her scent curled around me like a warm blanket. "So you want me to check in with you when I get back to town?"

"For starters." I didn't want her to go out of town in the first place, but I'd start at increased communication. "When are you going out of town again?"

I hadn't backed off, but she didn't push me away. She chewed on the inside of her cheek before she said, "I don't know. I mean, what's the point? I know it's only been a couple of trips, but how many creeps like the one I punched will I have to go through to find someone decent?"

Unless she opened her damn eyes and saw me standing right here with an engorged dick and a libido that hadn't turned off since I'd laid eyes on her. "A lot. Those places probably have a higher creep count cuz they're out hunting too."

Her mouth formed a troubled line. "I'm not on the hunt. I just want to live a little, but I can't help but feel so ignorant compared to everyone out on a Saturday night in the city."

"Maybe an orgasm would help?" Once the suggestion was out, I couldn't take it back.

Pink dusted her cheeks. "It's not that. I've had orgasms."

I couldn't squeeze my eyes shut and groan. Had she been getting herself off a couple of walls away from where I had been beating my dick into submission? "From a guy?"

The color on her face deepened. "Oh. Well, that's kind of why I'm going to the city."

Thank fuck I cockblocked her. "Sounds like you've got yourself a catch-22 there, Bright. You're too hesitant to get off with someone else since you haven't gotten off with someone else. That's where I can help." My lungs froze. No air moved. Would she go for it?

Her eyes widened as my suggestion sank in. "You?"

"I'm here." I was hard and willing. I rested a hand on the wall, half caging her in. "I'm a guy. I can do to you whatever you want me to in order to get you comfortable with someone else."

As far as compromises went, this was shitty. I would be priming her body to go look for someone else to fuck around with. But this was what she wanted. And I'd take fucking scraps if I needed to.

"You'd get me off?"

I couldn't tell how she felt from her tone. "Yes."

"Okay."

I cocked my head. Had I heard correctly? "What?"

"Do it. I think I just need to get over it once and I won't be so... scared." She said the last word through clenched teeth. "Now."

I left my head tilted. Had I fallen asleep while tossing and turning with a raging erection and dreamed this? "What?"

"Do it now."

Do it now. This was my chance to touch her. Her offer didn't feel like scraps. She was serving herself up on a gold platter lined with diamonds. And I was rock fucking hard.

My decision was instant. Here and now. I wasn't a big enough male to take her somewhere special. I'd been waiting months to get my tongue on her. "This is how it's going to go. I'm working my way down. You got me?"

"Just do it." She was strung tight, as if anticipating a punch. She'd made her mind up, and she wasn't turning back no matter how much it sucked.

Oh, my sweet Garnet. The only thing sucking would be me. "You're familiar with bases?" I tapped a fingertip lightly to her lips. "We've hit first, but we're still starting there." I dragged my finger down to her chest and cupped my hand over her boob. "Then I'll spend some time on second so you'll know if you find a guy who's lazy in bed. Tits deserve attention." Lower I trailed, dragging my fingertip over her stomach to rest at the waist of her jeans. "And then I'll spend some time here."

She vibrated with a different sort of tension. The sweet smell of her desire clung to me. She might think she would end up stuck with me, but I'd make damn sure to show that no one else out there could satisfy her like me.

I dipped my mouth to hover above hers. Her lips parted, her warm breath stealing over my skin.

"Ready?" I whispered.

A faint *yes* was lost as I captured her mouth in a soft kiss. I kept it light, promising, and when more of that fearful tension drained out of her and her desire bloomed stronger, I added pressure. Then my tongue. She stroked hers against mine. I tasted the toast she'd had for breakfast, and underneath was the unique flavor of her.

When she gripped my shoulders with her hands and widened her feet, I took the signal she was ready for more. Tugging her shirt up, I stayed resolute in my decision to keep her dressed. Would I rather have her naked and spread out under me? Hell yes. But anyone could walk into the library. It was fine if we were fucking around, it'd probably boost her reputation, but I wasn't going to put her in a vulnerable position.

Running my fingers over her bra, I made a mental image. Sports bra. Snug with a little lift, but not tight enough to choke her when I shoved it up.

I trailed my mouth down her neck, loving the little sigh that escaped her. She tilted her head sideways. Soon.

Soon, I'd be able to clamp my teeth on her neck. Right now, I had to build the foundation. I had to make her ready to beg for it.

I lifted my head. "You still with me?" I asked as I slid my fingers under the material of her bra. I stroked her pebbled nipples as I lifted the material over her tits. A shiver rolled over her body.

"I'm with you."

This was Brighton Garnet. She might be scared, but steel lined her veins. Gumption filled her organs.

I took in her round, high boobs with pinkish-brown nipples peaked so tight my teeth ached to sink into them. "I'm not undressing you, but I'm going to get you off good and hard."

She nodded, her stomach clenching. I bent, drawing her warm flesh into my mouth. A groan resonated through her chest into me. I flicked my tongue over her nipple, then gave her other tit my attention.

"Fuck, Brighton. I wish I could fucking drink you dry right now."

"W-why can't you?"

I looked up, keeping my odd angle. I couldn't reach these delicious mounds while kneeling. "As much as I want to bury my head between your legs, I can't risk someone walking in."

Her gaze darted to the door. She gave a shaky nod. "Could you... I mean..."

My chest nearly collapsed under the pressure of hope. "You want me to? Another time?"

She nodded. "It'd be like our training."

This time I straightened, but I kept my hand on a tit, rolling her peak between my thumb and fingers. I couldn't stop touching her. "You want me to teach you how to fight and how to fuck?"

"I already know how to fight." Her defensive tone was back, but it was softened by insecurity. "I hate feeling like everyone knows."

Being inexperienced at her age wasn't a bad thing, but in this town, it was a vulnerability. A point to stress to her nonsupporters. It was Brighton's job to know everything she could about her kind and her position. Fucking shouldn't be a part of it, but shifters liked sex. They liked experience. And they liked pointing out any kind of prowess they had that others lacked.

I could show her everything tonight. One night, countless hours. I could take her every way possible. I'd let her use me. But I didn't want her to wonder what it was like with someone else. I wanted her to want me as badly as I wanted her.

So I'd string out the pleasure. I'd leave us both achy and needy.

"Tomorrow night," I said, brushing my hand down her belly. "After dinner, you come over." I reached her pants and slowly unfastened them, giving her all the time in the world to change her mind—about this, about tomorrow.

She nodded, her hips rocking against me ever so slightly. The pressure behind my pants wasn't easy to ignore, but touching it made the need back off, as if my dick was satisfied with a maybe.

She gave a resolute nod as I skimmed my hand farther into her pants. She was tense again.

"Tell me," I demanded.

Her gaze flickered and a tremor ran through her. I was nearing her wet heat and I summoned all my restraint to keep from shoving my hand in her crotch.

"Tomorrow, we'll do this again."

"Do what exactly?" I was so damn close, but I moved at an infinitesimal speed.

Her inhale was shaky. "Tomorrow, you'll bury your head between my legs."

I jerked at her blunt words and my fingertips found her swollen clit. "I'll put my mouth on this," I murmured and slicked a finger through her seam. She bucked against my hand. "My tongue."

She drew in a shuddering breath. Her tits were still sticking out, her shirt tucked into her bra, but I spoke close to her mouth. There was no mistaking it was me talking to her. I wasn't going to be some faceless guy she got experience with. I was *the* guy.

I brought the tip of my finger back to her clit and circled. "I'm going to do this with my tongue." A moan escaped her. "And while my tongue is busy"—I adjusted my angle, no easy task thanks to her pants, and slid a finger inside—"I'm going to finger fuck you until you scream."

"Oh, god."

"My name, baby. Say it."

Her hooded gaze lifted to mine. "Ronan."

"That's right." My voice was thick, my cock on fire. I needed a release so badly, but it'd have to wait. Tomorrow. "Your voice is going to echo off the walls."

Her chest shuddered and her arms wrapped around me. Her hips had a mind of their own. She thrust into my hand. I hardly had to move. She rode me, her body tightening for all the right reasons.

"Ronan."

"That's it, let it go."

She widened her legs farther, giving me more room.

"Oh my god!" Heat exploded from her and her arms banded around me hard enough to cut off my air.

My body shook. I was a millisecond away from coming in my pants. I wasn't going to leave to change jeans and underwear right after I got her off. Grinding my teeth together, I tried to think of a hard workout. Dust on the shelves. The different shades I could stain trim. Anything but her velvet folds in my hand, her juice coating me.

Her grip on me loosened. I met her satisfied gaze.

She stiffened, shutters slamming in place. "Well. That's out of the way."

I withdrew my hand, hurt ricocheting through my chest. "Yep."

She tugged down her bra and straightened her shirt, then zipped her pants up. "I, um, forgot I had to talk to Selma. I should catch her."

Selma wasn't going anywhere. She never left city

limits. Brighton scooted around me, her face bright from the orgasmic flush. She breezed out the door, but I caught it before it shut.

"Brighton."

She flinched, but she turned around, her chin held high.

"Tomorrow night." I didn't make it a question. As always, the decision was hers. But I had to know. I could barely take knowing I might get to put my mouth where my hand just was.

When she didn't answer immediately, I calculated how much water I'd waste taking no less than five cold showers a day. Maybe I should make a snow fort in the backyard and sleep naked in it.

She inched her chin higher. "Tomorrow night."

~

BRIGHTON

I COULDN'T TAKE THIS. In just over twenty-four hours, I'd be on Ronan's doorstep so he could get me off again. If I'd experienced what he could do with a finger, what would his mouth be like?

His whole damn body?

"Brighton, are you listening?" Selma asked.

No. It was almost the end of my typical workday. I had planned to help renovate my office. A day of physical labor sounded better than contractors in my space or poring over spreadsheets. But alas, Excel won out.

"What'd I miss?"

"Was the weekend that eventful?"

The weekend had nothing on this morning. "No. I met with the youngest Peridot."

Her brows lifted. I had told her I'd talked to him but not that we had arrangements to meet. I didn't want her to get her hopes up. Worse, word might get out. I trusted Selma, but shifters had excellent hearing.

"He's just a friend." I clicked through the spreadsheet. "But we went our separate ways."

"Would he—"

"No." I knew what she had been about to ask. Would he be a good male to mate? "He's only a little older than me, and I don't know how well he fights."

"A human won't fight as well as a shifter," she said gently.

"I know."

"What about his brother?"

My stomach heaved at the thought. I didn't want Levi or Maverick. I wanted the male with the hot mouth and confident touch. But he didn't act like he wanted me. For whatever reason, he was holding back. And so was I. Especially after this morning, I'd have to be careful. I'd been putty. He could've molded me however he wanted.

If Camden had half the sexual magnetism as Ronan, I might've handed the entire clan over to him.

I wanted experience, but I couldn't lose myself. And that was all I wanted to do. I'd show up on his doorstep in a half hour if he asked.

A smart female would tell him this was the end. I'd have to get my experience elsewhere. This female didn't want to. This female thought the experience Ronan provided would be the best in so many ways.

This female wasn't strong enough to say no. Maybe once I sampled everything he had to offer, then I could search for another male to be with. Without the way Ronan intimidated me, I could be open. And maybe I could find someone who didn't tempt me to hand myself and the clan over. A male who wouldn't make it seem like my survival negated my parents' death.

Even if that male didn't want to mate me, I'd have built enough of myself that I wouldn't get bulldozed by the large Jade.

"No to Levi's brother. I've got some time, and Ronan is content to help with renovations."

"Isn't he interested? At all?" Selma ducked her head, searching my expression.

"He's not acting on it if he is." The bulge in his jeans said he was interested in something. He wanted more than sex in his relationship. So did I. But whatever that more was, I didn't possess it.

His parents had been so power hungry, and he'd been so infuriating when he'd first arrived. But only to me. The rest of the clan seemed to adore him. They seemed to prefer him. So his disinterest was for the best.

CHAPTER
SIX

B righton

IT WAS TIME. I left my house, my body awash with delicious anticipation, and as soon as I hit the sidewalk, I executed a precise left turn. I was doing this. A spontaneous explosion after cornering a male dragon shifter in the bathroom was one thing. Walking to his house in order to be stripped down and splayed open was my deliberate choice.

I reached his property, my anticipation pushing the boundaries of my skin. A familiar scent drifted on the frigid breeze across my nose. Sour milk and diesel. Stopping, I looked around. A chill that had nothing to do with winter crept into my body, clearing away the lust and depressing alarm buttons in my brain.

Camden.

I spun in a slow circle, stopping to glance at my house as if I remembered something. If someone was watching, they'd think I was absentminded. I wasn't, and I hadn't forgotten there was still a threat to my clan. But handling the sexual side of being a dragon shifter ruler with needs to meet had lulled me into a passive state.

Camden was no longer being hunted, but that didn't mean I should've quit looking for him.

Footsteps pounded on the other side of the block. Wayne rounded the corner, his eyes wide. "Did you smell that?"

Nodding grimly, I ground my teeth together. Any chance Camden was watching and thought I hadn't noticed was obliterated with Wayne's loud proclamation.

Ronan's front door opened, and he stepped out, wearing the same worn jeans he always did and a soft navy-blue hoodie that I only saw him in outside of work hours. His feet were bare, the only sign that he'd been ready for my arrival.

His green gaze speared me, a question lingering deep in their depths. He slid his gaze to Wayne, and his eyes narrowed. When his nostrils flared, I knew he smelled what had caused the tiny commotion outside his house.

Taking the steps down without bothering to put shoes on, hard energy swirled around him. Was he pissed our night was interrupted?

I was. I would gladly rip each limb from Camden's smug body as payment for the delay in the pleasure Ronan could give me.

"Wayne, call the rest of the council," I said. Our chance at surprise was gone. I had to go on defense. "I'll start searching Main Street."

Wayne regained his composure, his eyes flinty. I had always liked him, and I hoped he and Jimmie and Kiva weren't plotting against me, but I hadn't seen him bristle against an order like tonight. "What about your house? Is it safe to leave it alone?"

"The security is on." Security was always on.

Wayne searched my face, as if trying to understand what I meant. Selma knew the lengths I had gone to equip my house with security. I hadn't felt the need to inform the rest of the council when I wasn't completely sure who I could trust. They worked for the clan, and I had to answer to them in regard to clan matters, and vice versa. But my personal life was different.

"I'll grab my boots and search the neighborhood." Ronan was already sprinting back to his house before he'd finished speaking.

I wasn't dressed for walking up and down Main Street after dark in the middle of the winter, but my lack of bulky clothing was fortuitous. I could strip down and shift easier if needed, and I would be less hindered if I found Camden and had to fight without shifting.

In either form, I was ready for that bastard.

Trotting the rest of the way down the sidewalk and around the corner, I refused to dwell on what I was missing. My safety and the security of my entire clan came first.

I caught traces of Camden's scent as I jogged the last hundred yards to the corner of Main. His scent lingered stronger but intermittent in the air. Rounding the corner, I headed straight for the city council building. Selma lived on the second floor, and I wanted to check on her.

I took a deep inhale outside the entrance. There was

no trace of Camden. Pushing inside, I combed through the first floor, then jogged up the stairs to the second.

I knocked on her door. "Selma?"

She opened the door, the flyaways of her gray hair glowing in the pale lamplight. "Brighton? I thought I heard you rummaging around downstairs."

We were so close she knew the cadence of my footsteps. "We're catching bits of Camden's scent outside. I'm searching up and down Main, and Ronan's hunting through the neighborhood." Garnet River was so small we didn't need much more manpower than that.

Selma grabbed a sweater from the hooks by the door and stepped into her boots. "I'll go with you."

We finished clearing the council building before going back outside.

Jimmie was running down Main. He skidded to a stop. "Have you searched all the buildings?"

I shook my head. "City Hall is clear. I'll check the café next." Camden might've been making a good run.

"I'll clear the post office." He jogged across the street.

One by one, we swept through each business. One of the security measures I had taken after my family hoard was returned was to increase security of all the dedicated Garnet River facilities. Every building under renovation had cameras and electronic access pads. I knew all the codes. Ronan had access to most, thanks to his work with the contractors, and Selma could get into a few.

As expected, each building was empty with no signs of tampering. The diner had closed an hour ago and was untouched. The library was locked tight. With Ronan's scent all over the building, I doubted Camden would go near.

Jimmie stepped out of the post office and gave me a thumbs-up. "Want me to clear the gas station?"

"Already done," I called back.

I stood on the sidewalk outside of the library. Ronan was jogging down the street. From the consternation on his face and his rushed but nonemergent gait, I knew he'd found nothing.

He slowed to a stop. "All clear." How did he feel about Camden's interruption? Relieved? Frustrated? Glad to have something else to do besides me?

The streetlights cast shadows across his hard features, making him seem more dangerous and aggressive than he was. Or perhaps I was seeing him as he really was. The unrelenting Jade who had been rumored to use violence to get his way.

I hadn't seen that side of his personality. Did it even exist?

It didn't have to, not with me.

Ronan and Selma were staring at me, waiting for me to decide the next move while I'd been pondering Ronan Jade. I couldn't afford distractions. Forget anything sex related. I had to stay sharp. I had to act like the ruler I was.

"Selma, go back home but keep watch. I'll shift and search our surroundings. If we smelled him, then he hasn't had much time to get too far away."

"He might've flown," Ronan said, eyeing the dark sky. With thick cloud cover and no moonlight, it was a perfect, if cold, night for flying.

"I still have to comb the woods."

Ronan dipped his head. "Two of us can cover more ground."

Having his help searching the trees would be beneficial. We could hunt in either form on a night like tonight. To be safe, I'd hunt in my dragon form. The night was still going to end with me getting naked.

~

RONAN

KEEPING my steps from crushing through the snow and announcing to the entire woods I was coming proved difficult.

I was supposed to be buried between the legs of the sexiest female I'd ever seen. I'd never wanted someone so badly, nor had I waited so long to feel the sweet squeeze of a female's body around mine.

Camden was going to die for this.

Whether it was from my sexual frustration or my desire to shred every fiber of Camden's being apart, I canvassed my half of the woods in increasing arcs. I searched farther and wider than Brighton and I had discussed when we'd first marched to the tree line.

And I'd found nothing. A night of pleasure, hearing my name spill from Brighton's lips as her release coated my tongue, was ruined. For nothing.

I flexed my leathery wings. The jade sheen over the scales helped me blend against the shadowed white and brown of the snow in the trees gone dormant for the winter. If a human was on foot, and they weren't, or I'd have smelled them, I would only look like a hulking shadow, as if some of the trees had maintained their green leaves.

Brighton probably fit into the surroundings better

than I did. Her reddish-brown garnet sheen over her scales would make the trees look like they were alive as she moved.

I was missing that view too. Fucking Camden.

I lumbered along an old deer trail. My dragon scent would linger and keep deer off this path for weeks, but I couldn't risk snapping through branches, injuring the trees, and alerting Camden I was on the prowl.

I came to a fork in the trail. The left angled toward town, and the right side led deeper into the woods. Since I had energy to burn and a whole lot of temper to spare, I pounded down the path that took me farther away from Garnet River.

I tucked my wings close to my body, ducked my head down, and slowed my progress. Clearing my nostrils and inhaling, I filtered through as many of the scents as possible. Deer, fox, the natural decay of underbrush and leaves, and the dusty smell of snow. Nothing out of the ordinary.

Had Camden flown? Had he buzzed the town? The winter night was cloudy with little moonlight poking through. Camden's coloring would be the darker green of a typical dragon. He wasn't from a ruling family, no matter how badly he wanted to take over. He wouldn't have a jeweled sheen over his scales.

I could take to the air, but I was pissed enough to make a silly mistake that could get me busted by prying human eyes. Still, my gut insisted I keep going.

Moving as stealthily as possible, I crept down the trail. I still made good time in my dragon form.

I was about to turn back when the faintest whiff of a campfire blew across my nose. Stopping, I kept my breathing even. Inhale. Exhale.

There. Under the remnants of an old campfire smell was the odor of stale dragon shifter. This wasn't the same scent of Camden that we'd caught in town. He'd been here, but it'd been a while. This stench was from a guy who'd camped in one place with no running water thanks to the frigid temperatures and no company. A lonely outcast marinating in his own bitterness.

The male had to live in his dragon form. He wouldn't survive these temperatures in his human form, healing ability or not. Our natural energy could only go so far and constantly generating heat to heal the body from frostbite and hypothermia would wear out even the strongest shifter after several days. Camden's been camping in the middle of winter for months, likely eating deer, or maybe the occasional moose, if he was lucky. And he'd been doing it far enough away from Garnet River to keep from being detected.

Unfortunately, he wasn't here now. Perhaps I should think of his absence as a fortunate occurrence. Brighton had announced she would be the one to handle Camden. She would be the one to end him. If she wasn't, it would affect her reputation. The town collectively had an uneasy confidence in her ability, relying on the council more than other clans. Brighton needed to be the one to defeat Camden, and the only way that was beneficial to her was death.

I snooped through the campsite, sniffing and snuffling through mounds of snow. There was very little clothing. Almost no cooking supplies. This wasn't the land to provide shelter. Rolling hills with little crevices or caves.

The hills around Garnet River were small and gently

sloping with some craggier areas. Why had Camden chosen such a flat stretch?

We wouldn't have looked for him here. I was several miles from Garnet River and it was winter. Dragon shifters had grown to like their creature comforts. On dark nights, when the moon was new and the night was black as could be, we might take to the skies, but in these temperatures, it wouldn't be for long.

But if I was a dragon shifter on the run, I would want to stay out of all shifter territory. Scenting the air, I didn't detect any other shifter presence. If I was avoiding all shifter kind, I'd also want to stay out of mountain lion, wolf, and bear shifter land. There was little protection here for animals. This was a piece of land inhabited by smaller creatures, or it was a pass-through for the larger variety, nonpredatory animals.

What looked like a crappy place to camp was actually Camden's best option. The Peridot clan was too far away to detect his presence, and he was close enough to Garnet River to keep an eye on things.

I walked through the site, swiping my tail over the ground behind me. If Camden returned, he would find a destroyed camp.

Take that, fucker.

It was time to return to town. I monitored the sky for several minutes. Flying would be the most efficient. I could get a dragon's eye view of the woods and maybe find Brighton. She wouldn't go home. She would hunt Camden for days straight like she did after the incident last summer when that bastard and his family attacked Venus and nearly killed her.

I didn't launch into the sky. Slowly ascending, I let the leafless treetops scratch along my wings and scales until I soared above them. Staying close to the highest branches, I monitored my surroundings for prying eyes as much as I did for Camden.

I was nearing city limits when I spotted movement. A smaller dragon, blending in as well as I thought she would, flew as close to the trees as me. She swung her head around, her reddish-brown eyes narrowing. I gave my head a little shake, enough to let her know I didn't find him either.

The male must've spent his time for the last six and a half months searching for new hiding places. If he was smart, and I was dismayed to learn he was smarter than I first assumed, he likely rotated through his hiding places.

A traitor willing to sell out his family and let them die for following him, but he hid like a coward instead of outright challenging Brighton. And the worst part was knowing that if he was the victor in a fight with her, the town wouldn't question his role as their new leader.

It was the nature of our people. Might made right. It was bullshit, but it all came to physical prowess even after centuries of blending with the human world.

Circling toward her, I remained low until I reached the training ground we often used. A clearing of trees made it a good landing and takeoff spot. I came in like I was going to land, then swooped back up to fake out any shifter lying in wait. Brighton did the same thing. We each swooped in and out, abandoning the clearing like we decided to land elsewhere, and then returned to touch down. As soon as my talons hit the snow, I shifted.

Brighton was on the ground. She folded her wings in and blinked at me. She wasn't going to shift in front of me. A gift to my sanity. Nudity wasn't something I could ignore when I wanted to bury my cock in the female so bad my scales throbbed.

"I found a campsite, but I suspect he has more. We need to get a team together to search in a larger radius from Garnet River than we have, and we need to concentrate on places that wouldn't have any other shifters of any sort. They might seem like horrible spots for the middle of winter, but he's been smart enough to do just that and stay under our radar."

Annoyance ran through her expression. In her dragon form, she could communicate nonverbally. Like right now, when she was warning me to back right off from making plans about what she should do.

"Those are my suggestions. If you want me to be sweet about it, it's not going to happen."

She bobbed her head, her big body taut and her wings fluttering out.

"You're not going back out there?"

She swung her head toward me, the question, *Why wouldn't I?* in her eyes.

"He's covered his tracks. You need to—" I ran my tongue along my lower lip. I didn't like to sugarcoat things, but she'd be extra touchy about her leadership role after tonight. "You should meet with your council. Tell them your plans, hear what they have to say, then order them to carry out your wishes." I shrugged. "That's what I would do."

It was what my brother Lachlan would do. And Deacon Silver, the dragon shifter leader of us all. He didn't know it, but my brother had emulated much of his behavior. A real leader. Not like our parents. I would do the same, only I wasn't doing it as a rebellion that would make my parents turn in their graves. I did it to keep from trampling Brighton's authority just like they would've.

She thought for a moment, then nodded. Giving her privacy, I went in search of my clothing. After I dressed, I'd walk back to town without waiting for her. She'd wait until I was gone before she put her clothes on anyway.

My plans had certainly changed tonight and for the next several nights. Dammit.

CHAPTER

SEVEN

B righton

IT'D BEEN a week since we'd hunted for Camden. Thanks to Ronan's insight and advice, we'd snuffed out three of his camping sites. The jackass was running out of places to hide. I refused to let up.

The memory of how he'd attacked me and Venus during a training session. How I'd been left with no choice but to abandon her to get reinforcements from town. Camden and his slicked blond hair and spotless jeans for a guy who was supposed to be aiding the town with his mechanic skills. He'd been fake from head to toe.

I returned home after another long night of hunting. Our search teams were rotating through day and night shifts, but I worked twenty-four seven, stopping only to catch a few snippets of sleep.

Selma had issued several warnings about running

myself ragged. *You can't be at full strength in the fight when you haven't had a measurable amount of sleep for seven nights.*

Her admonishments were irritating enough, but I was getting looks from Ronan too. The lingering glances full of *Are you sure?* Or *You know you don't have to do this?*

I did have to do it. What if Camden had swooped on the town while I had been in Minneapolis? What if he had done it the night Ronan had followed me? The town was vulnerable. I was vulnerable.

I'd been going to sate my own needs while Camden had been stalking Garnet River, perhaps me. I couldn't let it happen again.

I stripped my clothes off as I walked down the hallway toward my bedroom. I tossed them in the laundry and went straight to the bathroom. I flipped the shower on and stepped under the icy water, suffering until the spray turned warm. Once it bypassed lukewarm to scalding hot, my fatigue draped over me like a wet duvet.

I was so fucking tired.

I'd shower, eat, catch a few winks, and then I'd be back out.

I flipped the water off and dried myself off. I didn't bother hooking the towel around me since I was going to crawl right into bed. Food would have to wait. It wouldn't do me any good to fall asleep midbite at the table.

I opened the bathroom door and nearly shifted into my dragon. I dropped into a fighting stance until I recognized Ronan leaning against the hallway wall across from the door.

Heart pounding, I screeched, "Ronan!" Too late, I remembered I was naked. "What are you doing here?"

"We have unfinished business."

"I'm working as hard as I can." I reached for the nearest fabric. A hand towel. Frustrated, I slammed it back down on the counter.

Ronan's gaze lazily traveled down my body. "That's exactly the point. You're going at this too hard, getting obsessed. He can use that against you."

Uncertain of what to do, I crossed my arms but let them drop. This was awkward. "I have to find him. If this was anyone else—"

"I didn't agree to make anyone else orgasm. And that's what you need."

A fire raged over my body. Did I blush pink from head to toe? "That almost distracted me too much in the first place."

"Bullshit. It was because you were outside that night that you smelled him."

Insecurity forgotten, I planted my hands on my hips. "If we hadn't detected him..." I was about to argue that we might've never known Camden had been in town. He might've caught us off guard or tampered with one of the downtown buildings. But because I had agreed to meet with Ronan, I smelled him. "You know what I mean."

Ronan wasn't buying it. He deliberately lowered his gaze to my breasts. "Go stretch out on your bed, Brighton."

Shivers erupted over my skin. I didn't like to be ordered around. It was demeaning and could affect my reputation. But the two of us, alone in my house? My body had a whole different response.

"Go lie on your bed and spread your legs."

He was so commanding, I moved without thinking. I

went straight to my room, crawled onto my bed, but I couldn't bring myself to widen my legs.

Ronan stopped at the edge of the bed. He stripped his shirt off and undid the clasp of his jeans. His gaze stayed on my body the entire time. "When you get off"—he shoved his pants down—"you're going to roll over and go to sleep. And when you wake up, you're going to eat a hearty meal, one fit for a dragon. A dragon ruler. Because the rulers, out of all of us, know they need to take care of themselves when the whole clan is relying on them."

"The clan isn't relying on me. That's the problem. Half of them are rooting for Camden." I couldn't stop until I proved I was a better leader.

"Then show them you can relentlessly hunt that asshole while maintaining full strength. But enough of that." He kicked his clothing aside. "No one else is allowed in this bedroom tonight. This is about you, your experience, and self-care."

A three-in-one deal. My lucky night. As Ronan descended on me, I knew how true that thought was.

He didn't dive between my legs. He stretched out over me, his hard body a warm blanket that could lure me into sleep if lust hadn't hardwired every nerve I possessed. He claimed my mouth, warming me up until he plundered the inside.

It was either fatigue or desire that kept me boneless underneath him. I unconsciously widened my legs to cradle his body. The big, rigid length of his cock was pressed between us. A hot stamp of moisture was smashed onto my belly.

I was even angrier at Camden for making me miss this.

Before I could get too incensed, Ronan kissed his way

down my neck, then stopped at each breast until I was writhing against the blankets. Finally, he licked his way down right to my wet center.

A long groan left me. All the need, all the frustration, carried on the sound.

I widened my legs even farther, bending my knees and curling my fingers through his hair. My inhibition had vanished. It was the two of us in the shadows. The last week wasn't forgotten, but it was momentarily on pause until I did exactly what Ronan had ordered me to do.

Shamelessly, I rode his face, seeking to get more of his tongue, demanding more. He interpreted the thrust of my hips correctly and pressed a finger inside.

I anchored my heels into the mattress. They were nothing but a tether to the tangible earth. My consciousness threatened to swirl out of my body and float away forever until he thrust his finger in and out. Then I slammed into a wall of unadulterated pleasure.

"Ronan!" I didn't know how many times I called his name as wave after wave of the strongest, most intense orgasm I'd ever experienced rendered me useless.

"Goddamn," he said, withdrawing his finger from inside me. "That was fucking beautiful."

"Ungh," was all I could say.

His low chuckle was enough to send shivers whispering down my spine.

He grabbed his shirt from the floor and wiped both of us off before tossing it into my dirty laundry basket. The action felt as intimate as what we had just done together. I was about to wrap myself up in the cocoon of uncertainty when he reached the bed and pried the blankets away. "Crawl in."

The roller coaster of emotions pumping through me since opening the door to find him in my house, combined with the postorgasmic haze, left me disoriented.

"It's time for you to sleep," he said.

"What are you going to do?" I wiggled between the blankets and he covered me up.

He propped himself on his hands over me. "What do you want me to do? I can sleep next to you, or I can sleep on the couch? But I'm staying in your house to make sure you eat some damn food in the morning."

I pouted, something I never did in front of people. "You're pretty bossy."

"Just between us. I promise I won't be like this in front of other people."

A burst of adrenaline shot through me, and my eyes widened. "Ronan, you can't make that promise."

"Why not? It's what you're afraid of." Was there disappointment in his tone?

Broken vows were a death sentence to our kind. We didn't make promises we couldn't keep, or we'd be executed. "You're a Jade. Yeah, I was worried."

Grim resignation filled his eyes, and I wanted to snatch my words back. Had I hurt his feelings?

I had spoken the truth. To take back what I said would be a lie. But I had an olive branch of sorts. "You can sleep in the bed. The couch is too hard to get any decent sleep."

"The couch is fine." He placed a soft kiss on my forehead and left.

My last thought before I fell asleep was that I had messed up.

CHAPTER

EIGHT

R onan

I WAS A JADE. I tried to tell myself that she was resisting me because of her own experience and not who I was. I should've known better.

I also couldn't blame her. And it had been long enough since my parents' deaths that I didn't blame myself either. But damn. Had the last six months been for nothing?

Brighton was still sleeping. Despite the moodiness clinging around in my brain, I'd been able to fall asleep for several hours. If Brighton knew what was good for her, she'd sleep for several more.

She wouldn't. The chip on her shoulder when it came to Camden was too large. If she wasn't careful, it would topple her over.

She could sleep for several more hours, and then

she'd be pissed at herself and redouble her efforts. That would only lead to an epic mistake that could cost her the clan or her life, or both.

I rolled off the couch, found my pants, and yanked them on. In the kitchen, I searched her cupboards and her fridge.

Frying bacon and sausage without a shirt wasn't my favorite activity. A grease fire had taken out my parents. A good thing to happen to them. I'd like to think it wouldn't be good for me.

By the time I was dishing the food onto a plate, Brighton stumbled into the kitchen. Her dark wavy hair was tousled around her face. She'd thrown on a loose, long-sleeved baby-pink pajama top. No bra. Almost the first thing I noticed about her. Did that mean she wasn't wearing underwear? Her flannel pajama bottoms draped to the floor. She looked cute. Delectable. Too sweet for me.

I set her plate on the table and laid a fork next to it. "Eat up."

She paused, as if she was going to say something, but slid into her seat and started eating, taking steady bites, just short of shoving food into her mouth.

As the heap on her plate dwindled down, I added to it. Then I sat in the spot next to her and dug into my pile of eggs.

Once her food was gone, she slumped in her chair and groaned. "I needed that."

I nodded.

Her gaze stayed on me, but I concentrated on my bacon.

"About what I said last night—"

"Don't worry about it."

"But I am."

She wasn't going to drop it. I wiped my fingers off on the napkin and turned my attention to her. Every bite I had eaten weighed in my stomach like a bowling ball.

"What I said," she repeated, "about you being a Jade."

"You don't have to explain. I understand."

She put her hand on the tabletop between us. A silent command telling me to shut the hell up. "My whole life, I heard of your clan. How ferocious your parents were. And then my parents and my sister died, leaving me in charge. Then I feared that kids from ruling families like Jade would storm to Garnet River and destroy me. Even when your brother took over, I was still worried."

"You weren't the only clan ruler worried," I said gruffly.

"Yet you came here, and you helped. I couldn't bridge the gap between my childhood bogeyman to the sarcastically arrogant guy asking for nothing in return for his aid."

I was used to people thinking like her. Everything she had said before that last sentence was what I had expected to hear. But then she hit me with the last line, and I didn't know what to do.

"I have to be really careful." She withdrew her hand. I was tempted to snatch it back and hold it. "I realize you understand that, but I wanted you to know that I know you're different. Your promise still scares me. It's an easy one to mess up."

"It is." I meant to stand by my pledge. Yet what I said was between the two of us in the darkness of her bedroom. If I went against my word, no one else would know. My life would be in her hands. She could turn the broken vow over to her clan's council or mine for my fate to be decided. Maybe it would boil down to a *he said, she said* argument and neither council would want to make a termination decision, but it would ruin anything Brighton and I had grown between us.

"My initial reaction, though, stemmed from the time before I got to know you."

"It's important for you to trust me."

"I trust you with a lot. But I'm afraid to trust you with everything."

There it was. Was this it? She would tell me there couldn't be more between us. My family's legacy came with too much baggage. "I understand."

"I need time." She leaned forward, putting both elbows on the top of the table. "I need to learn to trust myself before I can put that much faith in someone else, otherwise all that old fear is going to keep me from my full potential."

When I had said I understood, I hadn't really. Her meaning was clear now. "Is this the 'it's not you, it's me' talk?"

She didn't laugh it off. Her expression remained solemn. "No. It means I'm young. And I'm scared. You're the only one I can trust to say that to."

Dragon shifters admitting they were scared was a rare thing. For a ruler to utter the words out loud, it was unthinkable. My parents would've cut her down just for considering she might be scared. But they would've cut her down no matter what.

"Does Selma know how you feel?"

She shook her head. "I think she's scared too. She'd be happy if I mated you tomorrow. But I can't be with somebody until this"—she thumps her chest with her forefinger—"is one-hundred-percent put together. It's a lot easier to be strong when there's no one else to dump everything on."

Her words were both a compliment and a confession. She thought I was stronger than her, and she also thought she would be tempted to lean on me too much.

Since she'd been honest, it was time for some truth of my own. "I want you, Brighton. I want to take you as my mate. I sure as hell don't want you experimenting with any other males. But I get what you're saying. It's more important to me that you're with me out of your own free will. My family forced enough over the years."

"Not your family. Your parents. You and Venus could be accused of being pushy though."

The corner of my mouth kicked up. "Pushy is better than brutal. Sometimes a Jade still knows what's best for you."

Her laugh was a delightful sound. "I'll give you that. My training was necessary." She fell quiet, her gaze intense. "You're really interested in me?"

"Since I first saw you."

She drew back. "No."

"I swear."

She let out a gusty sigh. "There you go again. But really? I thought you had almost zero interest."

"I sensed your resistance."

"You're hard to resist." She folded her hands in her lap and contemplated them. "I hated going to the city. I thought about you the whole time. But my duties come before my wants."

"I understand." I didn't like it, but I got it.

She pushed back from the table and took our dishes to the sink. "It's time I get back out there."

"If I may?" The pushiness she had just mentioned needed to make an appearance.

She turned and leaned against the sink, crossing her arms under her tits. "You may, as long as it's not telling me not to hunt."

"I'm not going to tell you that. But some leadership duties need tending to."

Her mouth formed a troubled line. "Like what?"

"I'm just saying it would be best for you to update Deacon. Even Lachlan. I know it's not a secret I'm talking to my brother about what I'm doing here, but ruler to ruler, some of the communication should come from you."

She thought about it for a moment. "Since I have his brother staying long term in my town, and everyone expects us to mate?"

"You don't have to tell him specifics. But I also think he's looking for an excuse to travel out here. Jade has a long way to go to repair relationships with the other clans."

"You're taking care of Garnet clan." A flush spread across her cheeks.

I wasn't taking care of Garnet as fully or as hard as I wanted to. No one said being a patient male wasn't painful. "He wouldn't mind talking to Peridot while he's out here. Word made it back to him that you and Levi were talking."

She ran her teeth across her lower lip. She hadn't liked how word had traveled to Lachlan so fast. "I should give Memphis a call too. It's been a while since I've talked with her."

I dipped my head. I had hoped she would make the connection if we discussed it.

Her eyes narrowed. She knew I had been leading her to such a conclusion.

I let a grin spread across my face. "See? I'm not always demanding." I lowered my voice, filling it with all the ideas I had for her body. "Only when you like it."

BRIGHTON

SITTING in my office for most of the day after Ronan made me slow down had been sheer relief and stubborn torture. But he'd been right, and he knew it. My people needed to witness me continuing to be a ruler while I was hunting Camden.

The council had backed off on their hunts, and most of the people in town went about their day as if nothing had happened. I had been frustrated, suspecting all of them to be working with Camden in secret. Why else wouldn't they seem worried that a shifter who had altered the trajectory of the entire town was on the loose?

Did my clan like how things were going? *They might not be worried that you'll vanquish Camden. They may be satisfied with the progress you're making and would rather live their regular lives. They might—and listen up, Brighton—they might be satisfied with how you're doing things.*

Ronan's answer to my previous questions rang through my head. Especially his question to me. *Have you talked to them? Not just relied on the council's interpretation of how the town feels. Have you talked to the people? Really talked?*

I hadn't. I'd been raised so isolated after my parents died, so defensive, that I hadn't made many friends.

I didn't need friends. I needed to have conversations.

I faced the door to my office. It was almost one in the afternoon. Ronan was working on the library. I had done an early morning search for more signs of Camden before coming into work.

The lunch crowd would be thinning at the diner. If I was going to talk to my people, this would be a good time to do it.

Gathering all my resolve and holding it close to my chest, I walked out of city hall and across the street to the diner. The savory smells of fried food surrounded me. My stomach rumbled, reminding me that I hadn't eaten since I left the house.

Ronan had been making breakfast each morning before he left for the library. And each night, he gave me different experiences—new positions, multiple orgasms, drawing out one single orgasm until I was a quivering mess.

He made it hard to hunt at night or in the early morning.

An older male shifter sat alone in the booth in the corner. I spotted him chatting with Selma often. She had been good friends with his mate before the female had passed away last year. Boris had always been kind, but as he got older, he censored his speech less. I gambled today he'd do the same thing.

"Hey, Boris."

His bushy brows drew together like he was irritated about the intrusion, and then they lifted in surprise when he saw it was me. "Brighton. What brings you by?"

I smiled and flattened my hands on my legs to keep

from fiddling with my fingernails. "I've been told all work and no play is making me dull." Since it was the truth, I hoped Boris wouldn't sense any different.

"You always were a serious girl." He took a long sip from his coffee mug. "And a hard worker. But whoever told you that is right. Ruler or not, you're allowed to have a little fun."

The diner had survived some tough financial decades. Cheap burgers and even cheaper coffee had kept enough people coming back to prop the doors open. But without my family's hoard and with very little tax revenue to pay myself with in my bogus position of mayor, I hadn't been able to frequent the diner. The smell of greasy fries had taunted me for years. Selma would bring a burger over once in a while, and I thrived off her generosity. I knew I could afford to live slightly more extravagantly than I was, but I hadn't been able to justify the cost. Until now.

It was worth getting to know my clan again. "I figured I should start talking with people. Find out how everything's going. It's easy to have a one-track mind when I'm in the office."

He chuckled and set his mug down. "Thought you'd start with me? Friendly enough face." His smile was amiable enough.

"Selma's always spoken highly of you, but I've always liked how plainly you speak."

He chuckled again, a mischievous glint entering his eyes. "Not many people say that."

Which was likely why he was alone in the corner of the diner. "You should hear what they say about me." I meant that as a joke, but he turned serious.

"Most of them speak well of you. Hopeful. But there are a few who are waiting..."

"For me to prove myself?"

He dipped his head. "The Millers weren't as well liked as you might think. But we've struggled, and some will go with whoever offers a better life."

"I'm not just offering. The town is improving each day."

The dark skin at the corners of his eyes crinkled. "I would agree." He leaned closer and lowered his voice. "But not everyone is smart enough to see it."

I nodded and let my gaze stray to the window. Only a few cars sat outside the diner. Boris and I were speaking quietly, and no one was sitting close enough to overhear, but the clangs from the kitchen helped conceal our conversation.

"Get what you came for?" He took another sip from his almost empty mug.

Somewhat. I needed to talk to more than him. I needed more than a general feeling. Mostly, I needed others to see me interacting and it couldn't be fake.

I liked Boris, but he was expecting me to leave now that I'd gotten his opinion. Time to prove myself. "I haven't had one of Wanda's mushroom and Swiss burgers for ages. Can I buy you a slice of pie?"

"I have never turned down free food in my life, and I ain't starting now."

After I ordered, I chatted with him about his family. He had two sons. Both had moved away, marrying females from other clans.

"How is Junior liking Peridot?" I asked. I'd forgotten how interwoven our clans were. I might not talk to them often, but my people did. No wonder speculation about me and Levi traveled so fast.

"He says it's improving under Memphis's leadership.

Kids are always less resistant to change, and she's no different." Memphis was older than me. "My boy says there's a sense of hope there that wasn't earlier." He speared me with a direct stare. "Kind of like here."

A surge of pride rose up. The teenage server slid my plate of food in front of me. I thanked her, and she blinked at me like I told her I was the road manager for a boy band.

"Can I get you anything else, Miss Garnet?" Her voice was filled with awe. For me?

"It looks great. I'm good, thanks."

The girl beamed and scurried away.

Boris chuckled, and I shot him a playful scowl.

"That's not something I'm used to," I mumbled.

"Well, get used to it. These kids were raised during some dark, uncertain days. And then you rose up and nearly the entire Miller family was wiped out. Shifters my age? We've seen a few things. But the young ones? They're smart enough to understand that it was because of you. The Silver brothers and the Jade family were here because of you. Keep doing what you're doing and that sentiment will grow."

"Those are my plans." I picked up my hot burger. "That, and kill the last Miller who's threatening this clan."

This time Boris laughed. "I plan to be around long enough to see it."

NINE

B righton

THE FOOD NESTLED warm in my belly, and my conversation with Boris left me cautiously optimistic. Tomorrow, I'd stroll through the grocery store and hit up some other unsuspecting soul for a little chitchat. I might unearth some animosity at some point, but I had to quit fearing it. Hate was out there, and it was best to know who harbored it.

I tucked my hands into the pockets of my puffy green coat and strolled toward the library as if the bitter wind kicking at my face didn't bother me. If there were young kids in this town who thought I was a badass, I didn't want to disappoint them. I should've left the coat in the office.

I stepped into the vestibule of the library, a double set of glass doors that would keep the energy bill from skyrocketing. Before I entered the main library through the second set of doors, I tapped the snow off my shoes.

Hearing voices, I quietly opened the door. Who was talking to Ronan?

"I just don't think the library should be the priority in this town."

I frowned. Wayne was on the city council, and he hadn't discussed any problems he had with me.

"It's not up to you, is it?" Ronan's tone bordered on hostile.

"But it's up to you."

"What do you mean?"

I had the same question as Ronan. What was Wayne getting at?

"Come on. We all know she's going to mate you. Who else is there?"

"There are two bachelor Peridots not fifty miles away."

My stomach clenched around my lunch. I didn't want either of the Peridot brothers.

"And they would probably agree the library isn't a priority. We shouldn't be wasting our precious money on something the kids can get online these days. We're already paying for internet services and infrastructure."

"Garnet River isn't paying for the library. Brighton is," Ronan said tightly.

"Well." Wayne sounded as if he still wanted to find fault. "Your abilities would be better utilized in the post office. That place burns through a thousand-gallon tank of propane in a few months. That's a huge strain on city resources."

Enough of this. I didn't bother trying to muffle the sounds of my boots on the wooden subfloor. "And that would be why I've asked Ronan to talk to the contractor about an energy audit for the post office. And also why we're considering consolidating some of the other city offices into city hall. We can bring in another business in the building they're in. Just like I put in my weekly updates." I tilted my head. "Anything else you'd like to talk to me about since I'm here?"

Ronan didn't spare me a glance. He pinned his hard gaze on Wayne while the other male nervously played with the zipper of his coat.

Wayne finally met my gaze, chagrined. "I recall seeing those notes."

"I hope so," I said, liberally lacing my voice was sarcasm. "And if you have any questions about the library, or comments about why I've made the decisions I have, come to me. That's how it works, right?"

"I'll go to my office and reread the notes. Did you have time lines attached?"

"When the contractor gets them to me, I'll pass them on." I had to give him credit, he wasn't backing down. He'd been busted trying to bypass my authority and appeal to a male he assumed would become the next ruler of Garnet River. A male he hoped would walk over me and freely take my seat. "Now, if you don't mind, I need to talk to Ronan privately."

"I'll take another look at my email." Wayne ducked his head down and scurried out the door.

Ronan did a slow clap.

I tried to maintain a scowl but ended up giggling.

"That was sexy," he said. "I have to say I could watch you put him in his place all day."

"You might have a chance to. I doubt I'm done with him. Jimmie's going to have opinions about the energy audit, but that place has drained too much energy this winter."

"Think he's pro Camden?"

I pondered my interactions with Wayne over the years. "No. He was incensed the Millers turned on me and attacked Venus. He's not pro me, at the minimum." I'd have to keep an eye on him. "How are things coming?"

"Did you come to check up on me?"

"No, I want to let you know that I had lunch with Boris. Talked to him."

"It's a start. How'd it go?"

"Enlightening." I shrugged out of my jacket and draped it over an old bookshelf Ronan would sand and polish later. "You were right. I need to do more."

"Three little words most guys never think they'll hear."

I rolled my eyes but chuckled. "What do you want for dinner tonight?"

He grabbed the pencil tucked behind his ear and scratched the side of his head. After a few seconds, he slid the pencil back in place. His tool belt hung low on his hips, and he was dusty from cleaning all the side rooms out so he could lay down flooring. "I can make something too. You don't have to cook every night."

"It's my place." And he'd been tackling breakfast.

An unreadable expression flickered across his face.

"Did I say something wrong again?" I asked.

He frowned, like he wasn't sure what I meant, but then he nodded. "When you said it's your place, it made me think that I've been neglecting my house."

"You're working here all day. Do you want to go home and wear the same tool belt for another few hours?"

His expression remained carefully neutral. "I left the

spare bedroom halfway done, and it's kind of driving me crazy having something unfinished for so long, leaving nothing but a mess to show for my efforts."

He meant more than he was saying, and I wasn't sure I was interpreting his true intention correctly. Were we unfinished and a bit of a mess? Or was he just sick of sleeping in a bed that wasn't his own after making me come every night while he gave himself no pleasure?

I drifted closer to him. "I appreciate what you've been doing for me."

"No problem." The two words came out gruff. He readjusted his work gloves. Antsy to get back to work or uncomfortable about what I had said?

"Why are you giving but not taking anything in return?"

The muscles in each corner of his jaw flexed. "I told you about my parents."

He felt it was his due to make amends for the way his parents had behaved. But it was more than that. "I'm not talking about Garnet River. You and me."

His gaze was guarded. "You said it yourself. You're inexperienced, and I want you to feel comfortable."

He was being stubborn. If he wasn't ready to discuss his motivations with me, I wouldn't push him. But there was a chasm between us I wanted to cross, and I could think of one route to take.

It was unconventional but something I had been wanting to do for longer than I cared to admit. "I am inexperienced. You taught me a lot—about myself, about what I'm comfortable with, and about pleasure. But so far, it's only gone one way." I closed the distance between us and gripped his tool belt. His body jolted like I had shocked him even though our skin wasn't touching. I unhooked the tool belt and laid it at my feet. "Can I do this for you?"

His gaze searched mine. We were close enough that I could smell more than the dust in the air, the lingering mustiness of the building, and the faint stain fumes emanating from the back. All smells barely undetectable to humans. But they mixed with Ronan's natural pine-covered-hearth smell and comprised the whole package of him. It wasn't Ronan without a little bit of sawdust.

"Do you really want to?" he asked.

I nodded and slid my fingers behind his waistband. His stomach tightened, and I held back a smile. "I've been too afraid to ask. I wasn't sure you'd want me bumbling around down there."

A long groan resonated from his chest. "Brighton, I'd rather have you fumbling with my junk over anyone else."

Anyone else? Surely, he couldn't mean that. But I appreciated the sentiment. I needed the encouragement.

My hands trembled as I undid his jeans. Pulling the flaps open, I tugged his underwear down and freed his massive erection. Some of my trepidation drained. I wouldn't have to worry about the awkwardness of a soft cock despite my clumsy efforts.

Growing bolder thanks to the throb of his hard-on, I wrapped my hand around him. I'd seen him naked, but I hadn't touched him. I had let him tell me what to do, too afraid to make a move and having no idea what came next. I had struggled to remain at the top of my clan, but as nice as it was being cared for in the bedroom, I'd rather have equality.

I needed to start giving too. Pumping my hand up and

down his long, hot length, I studied his reaction. It did not disappoint.

I had expected him to squeeze his eyes shut, whether I was giving too much or not enough, but his gaze was glued to my hand wrapped around him.

"I've seen males naked before, but I haven't seen them hard." I continued stroking him, feeling him pulse under my fingertips. "Are they all as big as you?"

A hard glint entered his gaze. "Do you want to find out?"

Had my question upset him? "No. I'm just wondering how lucky I am you've been my first with everything so far. It doesn't seem like any other male would add up."

Arrogant satisfaction crept through his expression. "That's been my goal, Bright."

I paused, still gripping him in my hand. "Really?"

"Just because you wanted to know what it was like with other people didn't mean I was going to play fair."

My hand involuntarily clenched around him, eliciting another groan. "I don't want to be with anyone else."

"Your actions then said differently."

"I went to the city for the same reason I talked about the other night. I felt like I should to protect myself."

"You'll never have to protect yourself from me."

"I know that now." I gave his cock another pump. "Ronan?"

His gaze was hooded. "Yeah?"

"I'm glad you followed me to the club." I dropped to my knees, caught the moment his eyes widened when it dawned on him what I was going to do, and I sucked the broad tip of him into my mouth.

This time, his groan was nearly a growl. He jerked his arms up like he was trying to find a wall or a shelving unit to grip. Instead, he ripped his gloves off, tossed them to the floor, and stuffed his hands in my hair.

I explored. There was no finesse; I didn't know what I was doing. But I learned everything I could about him—his taste, his reactions, and what he liked.

I pumped the base of his shaft and sank into a rhythm, licking my tongue to his tip, swirling it around, and stroking back down.

"I'm gonna fucking blow," he panted. "Pull away if you don't want to—"

I sucked him down harder, as far back as he could go, until he hit the back of my throat and threatened my gag reflex. I was inexperienced, not unknowledgeable. He exploded just as I relaxed my throat. I wasn't ready for the force. His body was rigid, and he was trying to control the jerk of his hips, but his climax was too powerful. His roar echoed off the walls of the library, drowning out my sputtering.

I had to release him to swallow and wipe my mouth before I made more of a mess on myself than he could've.

He was immediately on his knees in front of me. Drip rag in hand, he dabbed at my mouth.

Cupping my face with his free hand, he ducked his head to peer into my eyes. "You good?"

I nodded, struggling to catch my breath. "Just a surprise."

"I'll say. That was phenomenal." He stuffed himself back into his jeans and zipped that magnificent cock away.

"You're just saying that to be nice."

"Truthfully, it doesn't take much for a blow job to be good. Only an excessive amount of teeth would ruin it, but I'm sure some guys are into that." He rested his butt on his heels. "But I've never come that fast from a blow job before, Brighton. And I've jacked off at least three times a day."

I scowled and sat the same way he was. "I don't believe it."

"I swear to you I'm not lying."

I gave him a small shove on his shoulder. A playful move compared to the position we'd just been in. "You're being a little too liberal with your vows."

"I've never made one before you."

"Seriously?" Shifters didn't make promises lightly. But never?

"Nope. I didn't need to give anyone more of a reason to get rid of me."

Ronan Jade was nothing like I had assumed. He went from being a chance at a decent mate in order to help my clan to being a better potential mate than I could've hoped for.

I could seal this deal right now. We could mate anytime, anywhere. But I held back. After six months of stagnation, we were finally moving forward. This thing between us started with me not wanting to have the weakest card in the relationship. Yet I was beginning to trust Ronan that wouldn't happen. But now I wanted him to know I was with him because of who he was. Not because I had no other choice. Not because he was a Jade. Because he was Ronan.

"I was going to search the woods again in an hour. Want to join me?"

He cocked his head as he studied me. "Brighton Garnet, are you asking me on a date?"

"I took a chance that you'd like my style."

"There's a lot about your style that I like."

"All right. I'll let Selma know."

Before I rose, he tipped my chin up and claimed my mouth with his. He deepened the kiss until I thought he'd topple both of us over and strip us down. I hadn't given much thought about where I'd lose my virginity, but in the middle of a half-demolished library wasn't at the top of the list until now.

He pulled away, desire darkening his eyes. "See you in an hour."

~

RONAN

THE SUN HAD SET a couple hours ago. When I arrived at the area where Brighton and I usually trained, I waited for her to suggest we split up. She never did.

For hours, we hiked together. I had asked about her childhood running through the woods. She hadn't been able to hold back her smile as she talked about how she and her sister used to play hide-and-seek all day until her mom had to come sniff them out.

"What did you do when you were a kid?" she asked.

I sobered, the tranquil mood of our hike vanishing. "If I thought really hard, maybe I'd be able to come up with some good times."

"I didn't think there would be any other times with Venus around."

"The Venus of today, yes. She's relaxed and has fun. But back then? No. If we were caught laughing, our parents wanted to extinguish the sound. Laughter doesn't win fights, or some shit like that."

"That sucks, Ronan. It really does. I think you would've been a mischievous kid."

"Lachlan's the one that has a secret, shifty side. One time he almost got my ass beat when he told me to go to the toolshed and grab the weed trimmer." At the time, I hadn't found the situation funny, but a smile ghosted over my lips as I retold the story. "It was the middle of June, and our parents didn't give a shit about how our yard looked. Lachlan figured it was up to us to mow and tackle the weeds. But I didn't know he'd already gone into the shed."

"Oh, no. What was in there?"

"A big fucking wasp nest. Only it wasn't easy to see. You had to be in the shed long enough to let the door shut behind you before you heard the buzzing. And then the jackass had set the trimmer right next to it. So when I grabbed it, I disturbed the hive."

Her eyes were wide, and she was trying to hold back a smile. "Did you get stung?"

Laughter erupted, catching me by surprise. "No. I ran out of there, slammed the door shut, and chased Lachlan all over the yard with the trimmer."

"It wasn't on, right?"

I arched a brow, and she sputtered.

"My sister knew I hated spiders. I like them now. Excellent mosquito catchers, but when I was a kid? Terrified." Sadness touched the edges of her expression, but her lips curved up. "Every time we played catch, she'd roll the ball under the porch."

"Did you grow up in the house you live in now?"

She shook her head, and her melancholy crowded out more of the humor. "No, I lived with Selma for so many years. By the time I was old enough to want to take care of the house, it had been vandalized to the point of destruction."

"The Millers?" I wanted to go back to the night we hunted Camden's family down and saved my sister. I wanted to kill them all over again.

She nodded, her jaw clenched. "Just another reason added to the list of why I want to kill him."

"It'll come. The more you get on with your life, the stronger his urge to meddle will get."

She spun on me, and we both stopped. "You helped me see that. I've had a tendency to focus on one thing or all the little things, but you've really helped me find balance this last week. Being around you makes it all make sense."

What she said got to me. I could give her orgasms. I could make her feel more pleasure than she had ever experienced. But getting her to trust me? Making her feel secure around me? That was where the real work was. And I had done it.

The moonlight picked up the red flecks in her irises. "Should we shift?"

"What?" I was still glowing from what she had told me. I had almost forgotten why we were in the woods in the dark in the first place.

"There's too much moonlight to fly." If we were on the other side of town, it would be a different story.

"I don't think he would be camped between Garnet River in the cities, or between Garnet River and Peridot Falls. But I'm getting chilly."

Chuckling, I jerked my hoodie over my head. Neither of us had worn more than sweatshirts and jeans. The night was cold, hovering in the teens, but the trees sheltered us from what little breeze there was.

Automatically, I turned my back as I stepped out of my boots and jeans. I neatly piled my clothing on top of my boots and set them off the main trail. I didn't need a mountain lion—shifter or not—nosing through my clothing and getting my boots full of snow.

Keeping my back to her, I waited for the energy crackling in the air before I turned around.

The charge from her change washed over me. Branches crackled. This trail was way too small to accommodate our size, but we weren't exactly out here just to hunt. Tonight was more like a date than any other date I had been on. We'd talked. Really *talked*. I enjoyed getting to know her, and now we were naked. Still a lot like my dates, but even naked in snowy woods, I was having a better time than ever.

She started to move, making room for me to shift. I let the change wash over me, my bones lengthening, my jaw turning into a snout. Scents became sharper, my hearing more acute. Being this close to Brighton in my shifter form was a delicious assault on my senses.

She still smelled like her. Cinnamon vanilla. But the scent filled my nostrils and my taste buds throbbed, remembering her flavor on my tongue.

She moved slowly down the trail to keep from causing a ruckus that would wake the whole town. Since we were technically supposed to be hunting Camden, I tapped into my awareness, trying to ignore the alluring female in front of me.

Squirrels, birds, frozen leaves, and not-so-fresh snow filled my nose. No signs of humans, and no signs of shifters.

The trail looped through the woods. Deer probably would steer clear of this path for weeks until the foreign scent of dragon faded. After about an hour, we switched directions and angled back. I could stay out for hours, but my dragon legs would appreciate not having to stoop to get through cold, brittle branches.

Back at our piles of clothing, I shifted and kept my back to her. I was about to retrieve my clothing when a warm, tentative hand landed on my shoulder. I turned, forgetting the chill in the air. She was still naked.

"I'm ready." Resolve filled her expression.

"For what?" Weren't we returning to town?

Her hand heated as she slid it around my neck and pulled my head toward hers. When our lips touched, an inferno exploded in my body, hot enough to melt the snow in a fifty-foot radius.

She pulled back far enough to murmur, "I'm *ready*."

My dick understood the message quicker than my brain. An erection was already prodding her belly. "Here?" I might know what she wanted, but I still didn't understand.

She nodded. "It feels right."

In the middle of the woods? In winter?

She said she was ready, and that was all I needed. We'd waited months. This wasn't rushing it. I smashed my mouth onto hers and yanked her against me.

No. Something about this didn't feel right. I broke the kiss. "It's your first time. It shouldn't be a quick fuck in the dark."

"It won't be because it's with you."

I briefly squeezed my eyes shut. This female was going to kill me. "Are you sure? We can go back to your house. Or mine. We can do this right, in the bed, where it's warm."

She stroked her fingers down my cheek, making my

dick twitch. "We're both exposed and vulnerable out here. I feel closer to you now than ever."

I couldn't deny it. I hadn't talked about my childhood in years. And she'd coaxed out some good memories, something I thought would never happen. "I think I still have an old condom in my wallet."

Her eyes flared. Shit. She hadn't thought about protection. Biting her lower lip, she nodded.

After I got the condom out of my pants, I warmed it between my hands before I ripped the packet open and put it on. My body heat might melt the rubber, but the condom wasn't going to break from the cold. I wasn't going to create new fantasies that would keep me awake at night, ones of Brighton's belly rounded with our child. An accidental pregnancy would only interfere with the progress she was making. And with that bastard still at large, I wasn't putting her or a child at risk. Camden was the type of male who would target her when she was the most vulnerable.

But one day. If I waited years, so be it. It would be with the female I'd given my heart to.

"Come here," I growled. I lifted her, but I didn't impale her. I took my time exploring the warm depths of her mouth.

She shoved her hands into my hair, her hot, wet core clamping my erection between us. I groaned. If it already felt this good, I might need a snow bank to help me recover from the rest.

〜

BRIGHTON

· · ·

I HAD PLANNED THIS. Before we met at the edge of Garnet River and walked deep into the trees, I knew this was how I wanted the night to end.

My legs were wrapped tightly around his waist. I wanted to be connected to him, but he was taking his time, and I trusted there was a reason why. Not that I didn't enjoy my naked body flush against his, and I would never turn down a make-out session with him, but I was anxious to feel him inside me. I didn't want to just know what it was like, I wanted to know what sex was like with him.

Finally, his hands were at my hips, and he lifted me. Flexing my muscles, I eased down until the big tip of his cock was at my entrance.

"Take it slow," he said roughly.

I didn't want to. We had done enough together that I knew sex wouldn't hurt. But it would be an adjustment, and I didn't want him to worry. This should be good for him too.

He steadied my ass as I relaxed my thigh muscles. He pushed inside. A moan left me. I needed so much more, but I wanted to savor this moment too. There could be only one first time. I hadn't intended to save it for the right male, but that was what had happened.

Inch by inch, he entered me. His body trembled against me. He was holding back, and I couldn't wait until he could give me everything and I could take it.

"You feel so fucking good." The guttural sound of his voice sent shivers over my skin. I didn't feel the cold, and after tonight, when I thought of winter, I would think of this.

He was seated fully inside. I adjusted my hips, taking

in all the sensations. The fullness. How connected we were. And the demanding throb of my body.

"Is that uncomfortable?" he asked.

I shook my head. "I like it. But I need more."

His grip tightened on my butt cheeks. "Take everything you need, baby."

I rose up, moaning at the way he stroked out of me. He tipped his head back, his teeth clenched.

I eased down. Oh, god, this was so good. I went fast, probably too fast for my first time. I couldn't get enough. And when he released one hand to slide it between us and tapped a finger to my clit, I didn't recognize the sound that came out of me.

"More." I rode him fast and hard, and I exploded harder than ever. My cries ripped through the silence of the night and mixed with his deep groan. He pulsed inside me, spilling into the condom.

I didn't know how I managed to hold on to him, but he held me as I shattered in his arms.

His breathing was ragged, and his body was stiff like he had two-by-fours woven into his frame to keep him upright. A chilly breeze caressed my ass. I was ready to be nestled in a warm bed with him and do this until one or both of us collapsed.

With my cheek pressed to his, I asked, "Do you have more condoms at your place?"

R onan

THE MAIN FLOOR of the library was ready to be laid down. Over the last two weeks, I had done all the side rooms. I didn't know how I had the energy. My nights were spent thrusting into Brighton's willing body.

After our first night together, I'd had to make a condom run. Last night, I made another. I was going to have to buy out all the gas stations and department stores between Garnet River and Minneapolis.

I wasn't complaining.

A slight creak of the front door sounded. I was stacking all the flooring into strategic spots. My knee pads were strapped on, along with my tool belt. I was all ready to go, but I hated stopping to retrieve supplies.

Whoever my visitor was came at a good time. Unless

that was Brighton. There was never a bad time for her to show.

Wayne was walking through the library, his head bobbing like he approved of my work. "How's it going, Ronan?"

Again? Wayne never talked to me unless he had a gripe about Brighton. A complaint he never seemed to make to her face or in front of the council.

"Getting ready to lay some wood planks." I had gotten a good deal with free shipping on wooden planks. It would be durable and easy enough to change out planks if one got damaged. I didn't explain any of that to him. He didn't need to know.

"The energy audit hasn't been done yet."

"The contractor doesn't have an opening until summer. Brighton put it in her report."

Wayne frowned. "Brighton said it was because she wanted to wait."

She wanted to wait until the library was done. I had told her that these renovations were going easier than planned, but it did no good to start on the post office without learning where it was hemorrhaging heat. The roof? Insulation? Air leakage around the big loading door or the smaller doors? The old windows that were painted shut? Brighton didn't want to rush the work or the contractor, so she kept to the same schedule.

And I wasn't the one to ask. "If you got a problem with that, take it up with her."

"Jimmie asked if I had more details than he'd gotten. I told him I'd stop on the way to city hall. I thought I might find her with you." His mouth tipped up like he was giving me a congenial smile, but it came off as nervous.

"Seems you and our fearless leader are becoming close. Is the mating right around the corner?"

I wanted it to be. I'd drop my tools right now if Brighton came in and asked me to mate her. But fucking Camden was still at large. Brighton was driven to be the undisputed ruler of Garnet River. With the way Wayne kept hitting me up, and from the sounds of it—how Jimmie questioned her reports—if we bonded, a lot of the town might start acting like Wayne.

As long as she would be mine one day, I didn't mind waiting.

I hooked my thumbs over my tool belt, keeping my emotions steady. I didn't like people knowing how I was feeling and until I could trust Wayne, I wasn't giving him ammunition. The clan didn't need to doubt things were moving along with me and Brighton. "We're getting to know each other. We have time. There's no rush, is there?"

To his credit, he didn't hide his conflicted emotions. "I'd like to say no, but I wouldn't be the only one to feel better if she took you as a mate."

"Why?" I made sure curiosity tinged my tone. I wanted to know the answer.

"She's so young. Selma's done well, but after the Millers..." He shook his head, but I couldn't tell if his concern was for Brighton or himself. "Your sister saved her. If she'd been in those woods training with Selma?"

"Both are strong females."

"Not as strong as Venus." He gave me a pointed look. "Not as strong as you. You have experience fighting. We all know that."

"Because I'm a Jade?"

He nodded, oblivious to the insult. To him, it was a

compliment. I'd grown up fighting. To me, it'd been for no damn good reason, and it'd only served to isolate our family. I wasn't pushing Brighton.

"Your reputation alone boosts the clan."

"My reputation is from before my parents died."

"It's better than an orphaned girl who was raised by an elder."

"She can fight."

His expression wasn't one I was familiar with, but I'd seen dads aim this look at their children when they're making a point. "Her ability isn't talked about among every dragon shifter clan around."

"It will be." I said it with confidence I didn't have. Did I think Brighton was a skilled fighter? Yes. Did I think she'd get the chance to show it? At this point, it seemed like Camden would be a ghost between us forever.

"Ronan, she's young. She's been protected by the council. The town needs to see her do more than throw money at shifters and humans to fix up the town. She might be ready for Camden, but is she ready to face someone she knows who's broken one of our rules? Is she ready to carry out a termination order?"

"These are questions you need to pose to her."

He scoffed. "She won't say no. And the council aren't the only ones worried." He gave a final nod. His shoes scraped against the floor and the door squeaked when he left.

I'd have to tell Brighton about this interaction. About the questions Wayne had brought up. I worked on the floor for hours, stopping only for a quick sandwich I had packed that morning. After two more hours of work, my phone rang.

Groaning, I arched my back, then swiveled to sit on my ass. Lachlan's name was on the screen. "What's up?"

"You tell me. Why do I have Maverick Peridot asking me to call you off from Garnet River so Levi can mate Brighton?"

"The fuck he will."

"Apparently, Maverick has some bullshit story about when Brighton was in the city with Levi. He got in trouble and Memphis thinks he'll settle down if he mates. According to her, Brighton owes him."

"She owes him nothing. Not the time of day, not a quick hello, and not a goddamn mating." There was room for only one male between me and my future with Brighton.

"What the hell happened? I thought you said everything was fine, that you were only waiting on her fight with Camden until she mated you."

"Nothing's changed. That's still the plan." This morning everything had been fine. My grip tightened on the phone. "Fucking Wayne."

"Who?"

"A council member who talks like he wants someone other than Brighton in charge. He thinks she doesn't have the fortitude."

A heavy sigh came over the line. "Look, this isn't just going to go away. Brighton is a single female ruler. Levi is from a ruling family. And she's from a neighboring colony. She's easy pickings. I'm surprised they haven't tried before."

"But why are they trying it now? Levi didn't give off the vibe he was ready to settle."

"Maverick wasn't forthcoming. I'm heading down."

"You don't have to. She can tell him no." I'd tell him and relish doing it.

"They need to realize they're messing with Jade. You're in Garnet River at Deacon Silver's request. You're there because I supported the idea. You're still there because you've fallen for her. No Peridot jackass is going to interfere."

"If you come, it's going to look like Brighton still needs someone to stand up for her."

"We all need someone to stand up for us sometimes."

He had a point, but Lachlan wasn't the type to butt in where he didn't belong. "Are you just trying to get away from Indy?"

"Don't you dare go there."

I clenched my jaw. I knew his mate was a touchy subject, but my question was valid. "Does Brighton even know about any of this?"

The door to the library crashed open and a gust of cinnamon vanilla scented wind blew across my back.

"Never mind. I think she does."

BRIGHTON

I LISTENED to every word Ronan said about Wayne's visit and Lachlan's impending arrival, my temper rising higher until I feared the top of my head would explode outward and I'd become nothing but a tornado of rage. "He doesn't need to come."

"He's coming. I'm sorry."

I paced over the new floor. I couldn't even admire the

work Ronan had done. I was upset with him, his brother, and Wayne. How could Levi throw me under the bus like this?

I should've never gone to the city. "I'm going to tell Memphis no. I'm not mating Levi."

"We need to listen to her reason first."

I stopped, hurt ricocheting through my chest. He wanted me to entertain the idea?

He held up his hands as if he was trying to hold back the storm of my emotions. "Not because I agree, or because I think it's a good idea. There's something going on. And the more informed you are, the better you'll be able to fight this."

"There's no fight. I'm not going to mate him."

He stalked toward me. "I know you're not. Because you're mine. And as soon as you say the word, I will put my claiming bite right here." He brushed his finger over my collar.

A shiver caressed my spine. Only his touch could ease my anger. "I suppose it looks better if your brother is here to support us—as long as he doesn't interfere. And it can't hurt to tell the council you and I are waiting until Camden is taken care of because of attitudes like Wayne's."

He dipped his head. "I agree."

"It just makes me so damn mad. The last two weeks have been really good."

"They've been amazing," he murmured.

I stepped into his warmth, and he circled his arms around me. "Let them come. Find out what Levi's up to, or what his sister's up to, and figure out your plan then. If you get too focused on stopping them, you're going to stay on the defensive when you want to be on the offense."

"Are you telling me what to do?"

His chest moved with his soft laugh. "I believe the limit of the promise was in front of everyone."

"I guess... I kind of appreciate your brother coming. Between the two of you, it's nice to have someone I can turn to when my own council isn't the best choice."

His expression turned serious. "You're going to need to deal with Wayne's concerns."

If Wayne was concerned, so were others. "I know, but it's not like I can ask someone to break the rules so I can kill them." A shudder ran through my body. Killing those who broke our unbendable rules was a tragic fact of the job. The council had performed those duties until I was old enough, and thankfully, the town had been quiet. "The termination policy will come in due time. The clan will have to be patient."

"My brother can stay at my house."

An idea percolated in my brain. "Yeah, he can stay in your place. How about you move into my place?"

His brows popped. "That'll send a strong message."

"That's the goal. No one needs to know what we're waiting for." If Camden learned of the reason for the delay, he'd make sure he was never found. I would talk to Selma, but that would be the extent of it. The other three council members could wonder with the rest of the town what my plans were.

They can be on defense and wait for a turn of events like I was.

ELEVEN

R onan

WHEN LACHLAN ARRIVED, he came straight to the library. I was in the delivery bay polishing bookcases when he charged through the door from the library to stand on the steps staring down at me. "I can see why she keeps you around. That's a whole bunch of free labor out there."

"If this is going to be my new clan, then I should take part in the renovations."

Lachlan took the five concrete steps down to the garage floor. He roamed the perimeter, unconsciously checking the doors and exits.

There was only one large garage door, the door into the library, and another door leading outside. The garage door and the exit door both remained locked. I didn't mind the front door remaining unsecured while I was in the building. I didn't mind flaunting my confidence that no one in Garnet River could mess with me.

My brother's heavy boots hit the cement floor as he walked by each one of the bookshelves I had hauled into the bay to get sanded and stained.

He was dressed a lot like me. A hooded sweatshirt, worn blue jeans—only his didn't have holes—and work boots.

Squatting, he ran a hand over one of my finished pieces. "Not bad."

"It's a quick job, but the shelves will be lined with books. I didn't need it to be perfect."

He studied me, still in his squat. "I wasn't critiquing your work."

I lifted a shoulder. "Habit." Our parents had expected perfection out of everyone but themselves.

"Memphis here yet?"

"She told Brighton this weekend. It'll be her and Levi. Maverick will keep watch over Peridot Falls."

"Any idea what they're up to?" My brother was a straightforward guy. He had all the uptight traits of the oldest child with the rigidity of a natural-born ruler. He didn't play games, and he didn't tolerate them.

"Something that serves Peridot." I picked up the sander, ready to turn it on, then set it back down. "What bugs me about this whole thing is that Levi seemed cool—with Brighton and with me and Brighton. He seemed on the selfish side, but not unlike any other guy in his midtwenties."

Lachlan rose, his expression introspective. "No male shifter in his midtwenties wants to settle down unless he's head over heels in love."

"Definitely not how he acted in regard to Brighton."

He thought for a moment, then nodded. "Your girl-friend doing a wait and see?"

"Nothing else she can do without making more problems for herself." The last thing Garnet River needed after the Miller debacle was beef with the closest dragon shifter clan.

Faint footsteps down the hallway caught our attention. Neither of us said a word as we watched the door. It wasn't Brighton's cadence. Someone bigger.

The door opened to reveal Jimmie. Surprise crossed his face when his gaze landed on Lachlan. "Oh. I didn't realize you had company." He stepped all the way in and let the door shut behind him. "I heard some girls in the café discussing a new male shifter coming to town."

"Jimmie, this is my brother, Lachlan." I didn't have a problem with his visit, but after Wayne, I was on edge wondering why Jimmie was here.

Confusion and what I'd describe as dismay passed over Jimmie's face. "Brighton didn't say we were getting visited by another clan's ruler." He rushed down the stairs and stuck his hand out to Lachlan.

My brother shook his hand but didn't address the comment Jimmie had made.

Jimmie looked between me and my brother, like he was waiting for an explanation. We returned his questioning glances with a stare.

"What can I do for you, Jimmie?" I asked.

His gaze darkened for a heartbeat before he clapped his hands and scanned the bay. "Well, I heard you were making great progress with the library. I'll be honest, I wanted to see for myself the kind of work you're doing." He bobbed his head and jerked his thumb over his shoulder. "That's some quality work out there. Is this what you do for Jade Hills?"

"I dabble." I had refinished my house in Jade Hills, and a few shifters had hired me for side jobs, but I had to cut my teeth on getting the old armory turned city hall building renovated into the current century.

"I'd say you do more than that." Jimmie propped his hands on his hips and bobbed his head again. He struck me as a guy who would be a science teacher if he lived in a larger city. Brighton had said he used to teach at the small school in town, but he had stepped down when he took the seat on the city council about a decade ago. "I know Wayne has been bugging you about the post office. Brighton hasn't shared her exact plans with that building yet, so I admit to being a little nosy. I was wondering if you were going to take on that project yourself."

He was smoother and definitely more subtle about digging for information. If I was a guy swayed by compliments, I'd probably fall for it. But Brighton's interests were my best interests. "We'll have to see."

His chuckle was good natured. I took a deep inhale, trying to detect a lie or some kind of negative emotion, but Jimmie was neutral.

"Have you come up with any ideas? Just in case? I would love to hear any and all thoughts about the building."

Was the post office a tool used to pick away at Brighton? Was there something about that building Wayne and Jimmie knew that Brighton didn't? "I haven't given it much thought. It's an important business in town, obviously, but it won't be used by the public like the library. Structure is more important than aesthetic, and that's where I'd need to turn it over to the expertise of a contractor."

I wasn't lying. The contractors that had worked on the city-owned buildings in Garnet River had done a general check on every business Brighton planned to renovate. The post office was structurally sound, but I was the wood and surface materials guy. I wasn't an HVAC guy, and the post office would need a lot of work in that area.

My brother watched us, quietly studying our interaction. I was interested to hear his insight on the exchange. Jimmie seemed nice enough, but there was something about his visit and his questions that weren't sitting right in my gut.

"I'm sure the structure is fine. That old building has been through hell and high water. My father was the postmaster before me. That place is my second home." Jimmie laughed with a little squeak on the inhale. If I wanted to hang up a poster showcasing the resident nerd of Garnet River, Jimmie would be proudly wearing a lab coat on the front. "I'll leave you two be. Sorry for the interruption, but a guy's gotta be nosy, you know."

I chuckled more because it was expected of me. It wasn't a bad thing to stay on the good side of a council member since I hadn't been helpful with Wayne.

He nodded at Lachlan before he left. My brother and I said nothing as we listened to his footsteps recede down the hallway. I strained to listen for the front door to open and close. Satisfied the male was no longer in the library, I met my brother's gaze.

"What do you make of that?"

"His delight with how the library's turning out

seemed sincere. I didn't sense anything off, but that doesn't mean his interest was actually the library."

"But he was more likely interested in what he would find out from me," I finished for him.

He dipped his head, agreeing.

"I'll have to see what Brighton makes of his visit."

Dammit. She had not one but two council members whose motives she needed to question, but she also had the impending arrival of Levi and his sister.

Then there was the festering topic of Camden. The longer we didn't deal with him, the more toxic he got. But until he showed his face, there were plenty of other issues.

~

BRIGHTON

I HAD DISCREETLY WATCHED out my office window as Memphis rolled into town with Levi in the passenger seat. Her red Dodge Ram stood out like a shiny diamond in a pile of dead branches.

When was the last time a Garnet River shifter bought a new vehicle? My new-to-me car was still ten years old.

Ronan tapped his fingertips together in the chair across from my desk. I had asked him to be here when Memphis and Levi showed up. Yesterday, he brought all his clothes to my house. The gazes of everyone staring out the window up and down the street had burned into my back as I held the door open for him.

With the arrival of Levi and his sister, the town was probably buzzing worse than a million bumblebees.

Selma's voice echoed down the hall, her volume higher than normal. Her way of announcing the arrival of our guests as if I'd been able to lose myself in other projects.

She tapped on my door. If nothing, we were putting on a good show that I was busy. Hopefully it would at least look like I hadn't been anxiously awaiting their arrival since I woke this morning.

"Come in," I said, barely raising my voice.

The door swung open to reveal Memphis Peridot. Her short, pitch-black hair was swept over to one side, revealing a trendy undercut I had seen several women at the club have. Just like her pickup, her fashion blew away any clothing I owned. Rhinestones lined the seam of her jeans, and if she turned around, I wouldn't be surprised to find designs on the back pockets. Like most shifters in the middle of winter, she wasn't wearing a coat. Her loose cowl neck sweater still managed to hug her ample breasts and pool around the flare of her hips, giving her an hourglass figure.

Levi flashed a guilty smile from behind her shoulder.

Sparing him little more than a quick glare, I calmly said, "Have a seat."

When I arrived at my office this morning, I made sure there were three chairs in my office. Earlier this week, I'd ensured the contractors wouldn't be around. The main floor room that had once been a dining room at the saloon was getting converted to offices, but the work could wait for a couple of days. In case things went south, I didn't want collateral damage.

Selma had assumed she would be in on the meeting, but after I explained, she understood. It was time to cut the cord between us. She was no longer my guardian, and she was still a council member. I couldn't have just her hearing Memphis's excuse for why I should mate her brother.

Memphis regarded me coolly before she strutted to the chair closest to Ronan. My first inclination was to bristle. Was she trying to make me jealous? But the seat she chose happened to be directly across from me and more appropriate for her station. I didn't know Memphis well, but she had never seemed like a female who would take the long route when she could crash through the obstacle instead.

I didn't have to worry about how I was going to phrase my questions. She waited for the door to close before she spoke. "I know you're wondering why I think you should mate Levi when you've got this guy here."

"I am."

She held up a finger with a yellow-painted, sharp-tipped nail. "One, I didn't know you two were banging each other senseless. All I had heard was that it was a whole lot of nothing between you and him."

I forced myself to breathe evenly lest a blush creep up my face. Ronan's smell was all over me and vice versa. Any shifter would know what we had been doing together. They wouldn't have needed to watch him haul his belongings into my place.

Levi snickered, and Memphis cut him a quelling glare.

She ran her tongue along her teeth. "But the fact of the matter is... you haven't mated with him yet. You're still single, and you're a female from a ruling family. You and Levi get along, and you owe him."

Levi winced and shifted his gaze to the far wall. His jaw was tight. What was the story?

"That's where I'm confused," I said. "How exactly do I owe him?"

Her gaze jumped between me and her brother. "He agreed to meet you that night. The night you decked the human."

That asshole?

"Grinder?" Ronan asked.

"I didn't make introductions," she said succinctly.

"Yes, Levi agreed to meet with me. That was the extent of it. We parted ways shortly after." When Ronan had appeared and I'd kissed him within minutes of his arrival.

"Oh, but it wasn't. Because that guy saw him with you, he thought he'd follow him to find where you are." She rolled a shoulder. "Creeps hold a grudge."

"That guy didn't even know my name. How could he attempt to stalk me? He knew nothing about me."

"Only that you met Levi, and therefore, Levi knows you."

The creep must've been watching the club before he picked his targets. He'd seen me with Ronan and Levi, yet it hadn't stopped him. He'd hoped to drive me out of the club and gambled the guys wouldn't follow.

It was disturbing to hear some human was obsessed enough to harass my friends, but her insistence I mate her brother still didn't make sense. "How does some human who doesn't know the definition of '*no*' connect to the reason why you're here?"

She cut a look at her brother, her lips in a flat line, then directed her stare at me. When she spoke, her voice was low. "I had to kill him."

"Shit," Ronan breathed.

After the shock wave passed, I continued to try to

make sense of all the information she'd given me. "That sucks, but it doesn't answer my question."

Killing humans could expose a clan. Human law enforcement often wanted answers they were better off not knowing. The danger was why our laws were irrefutable. If they were broken, the shifter paid with their life. One shifter for the safety of the clan. Memphis had done what my council questioned my ability to do.

"Our council is upset. They blame Levi for leading a human to our clan. A human that saw too much because of you."

"I'm not to blame here."

She held up that infuriating finger again. "My brother was there that night to help you. And when a human saw him shift in the middle of nowhere—nowhere a human should be—he saw what he shouldn't have, and he swore to my brother—a brother from the ruling family—that he would tell everyone if Levi didn't tell him where you were."

Now it all made gruesome sense. The human had made a vow to a shifter. No human was supposed to know about our kind. No one was allowed to tell other humans about our kind. That alone was a death sentence before he even had a chance to break his promise.

"Peridot Falls already has me, and there's Maverick if anything happens to me. Levi's behavior is viewed as a liability. The council wants him terminated."

"My sister," Levi finally spoke, his voice a fine wire of barely restrained emotion. "Has mollified the council by promising to mate me off. I had no say, otherwise I would never have proposed this ridiculous plan."

"You're alive, aren't you?" Memphis snapped.

"You had no right—"

She turned the silencing finger on her brother. "I would rather make your life a little uncomfortable than be faced with killing you."

"It's not just my life, Memphis. We've been over this." Levi stabbed a finger in my direction, then Ronan's. "There are two other shifters here you're messing with."

Her hard, determined expression wavered. I witnessed a crack in Memphis's armor. She had made the decision, and as a ruler, she was carrying it out. But now, she was faced with the consequences. Our circumstances were nothing alike, but I felt like I was looking into a mirror, showing me my future.

I hadn't killed anyone yet. But in my position, it would be my job to do the same as her. If a dragon shifter, or any shifter in Garnet River's vicinity, decided not to mate by the time they were thirty-five, it would be my job to terminate them. I would have to kill someone who had done nothing other than decide to stay single. But without the mating bond, our aggression could grow unbridled until we were a threat to our kind. That was the trade-off our people had made centuries ago when they had agreed to live in the human form. There were consequences to breaking our rules.

I was that consequence.

Memphis would've been that consequence for Levi. He had unintentionally broken one of the most major rules of our kind—never reveal our secret to a human who wasn't a mate—but he had unwittingly revealed himself. That was punishable by death.

"There's got to be something we can figure out," I said, exchanging a glance with Ronan. I read into his expression as much as I could. He empathized with the brother and sister pair, but like me, he wasn't willing to forgo his happiness to save Levi's ass.

Memphis threw up her hands. "I'm all for ideas. But it has to be good enough to mollify my council."

I had nothing. "There's a solution; I refuse to believe there isn't. But it's going to take time. You two can stay here. We'll make it look like we're having a tug-of-war about who I'm going to mate, and in the meantime, we'll search for someone else who'll be a good match for him."

Memphis's eyes narrowed. She crossed her arms and twisted toward Ronan. "You're quiet. What do you think of all this?"

"Levi isn't getting my female." Ronan's growl went straight to my core. It was even more exhilarating when he made his claim in front of people.

"Told you it was like that," Levi grumbled.

Memphis shot him a glare before turning her attention to me. "We can stay here, do what you said, but you can't mate with this guy until Levi finds someone."

Darkness settled over Ronan's expression. Did that upset him?

It was disappointing, but I still had the lone surviving Miller to deal with. Putting off my mating to help save Levi's life seemed a lot more noble compared to that. "We'll make that work."

Ronan jumped out of his chair, startling all of us. "I'll be at the library." He stomped out.

"He took that well," Memphis said dryly.

I wanted to rush after him, but a frantic female asking why her male was upset wasn't exactly the leadership example I wanted to give.

"Let me get Selma. We'll figure out a place for you both to stay." I tapped out a message, asking Selma to come to my office. "Also, Lachlan Jade is here. He came because of his brother."

Memphis let out an undignified snort. I liked her better for it. "I'm sure he claimed it was his brother. He's probably running from his mate."

"Memphis," Levi hissed.

I didn't mind the extra gossip. Memphis had just revealed she was more in the know than me. I had been sleeping with Lachlan's brother every night for a couple of weeks, and I didn't know Lachlan was having issues with Indy.

She rubbed the back of her neck. "Indy and I have a mutual friend. I know more of Lachlan's business than he wants me to." She bobbed her head. "It's a good time."

Selma knocked firmly and entered. I explained that Memphis and Levi would be Garnet River's guests while we figured out the mating situation, I mentally breathed a sigh of relief.

Memphis was the type of ruler other rulers would do well to maintain a good relationship with. If Levi didn't want to mate me as much as I didn't want to mate him, this could have been bad.

Selma perched in the chair Ronan had vacated. My mind kept wanting to turn to Ronan. My feet itched to chase after him. Maybe some cooling-off time was for the best.

"We have the house the Crenshaws put up for sale," Selma said. "We could offer to rent it."

"Yes, to renting the house. No, to Garnet River footing the bill." Memphis turned her superior stare on me. "Peridot pays their own way."

Internally, I'd made notes of the way Memphis spoke and her mannerisms. She oozed confidence. Exuded control. She spoke as if she ran the town and everyone knew it.

I matched her energy. "I'll accept your offer to pay. The house might still be furnished. Kim Crenshaw passed away a month ago, and the family wanted to wait until the snow melted before they cleaned it out."

Levi leaned forward. "She didn't die in the house, did she?"

Memphis rolled her eyes. "There's no such thing as ghosts."

"Says someone in a roomful of people who can turn into dragons." Levi waited for my answer.

Memphis spoke first. "I'll amend what I said. There are no dragon shifter ghosts. We have better things to do after death."

I was tempted to smile at their sibling bickering. It reminded me of how my sister and I used to act. Something I didn't do often enough. "No, Kim passed away in the woods. She wanted to shift into her dragon one last time."

Approval rang in Memphis's eyes. "That's the way to go."

A fond smile graced Selma's lined face. She must sense the easiness between us compared to when Memphis and Levi first entered. I wanted to tell her the full story, but that would have to wait.

"Selma will get you settled." I rose. "She'll show you where I live, and you can stop by here anytime."

Mischief gleamed in Memphis's bright eyes. "I think you should be the one to settle us in our new digs."

Levi's eyelid strip shifted shut, but he didn't argue. Right. Pretending.

"Selma will take care of you." I left without further

explanation. It would be best if I showed them around and added to the speculation for their council. But I couldn't. The hurt emanating from Ronan was churning in my stomach.

I couldn't help the delay, but I felt responsible nonetheless.

CHAPTER

TWELVE

R onan

I WAS SANDING BY HAND, using an amazing amount of self-restraint to keep from gouging the wood, when Brighton charged into the bay.

"Care to tell me what that was all about?" she demanded.

I continued to sand, a steady back and forth, going with the grain of the wood. This shelf would be the nicest out of the set after all the time I was spending on it. The library project that was moving at a fast rate had suddenly slowed down. I could milk working in here for several more weeks. It was better than being in public, making a show of trying to win the affections of a female who had said she wouldn't be mine.

"Ronan?" Her tone was softer than when she hit the bottom of the stairs.

"If you don't want to be with me, you can just say so. I won't lose control."

She frowned and crossed her arms. "What are you talking about?"

I abandoned my task. "You ignore me for six months, saying it's because of our age difference and the amount of experience I have. Then you get with me, but we can't mate because Camden's at large, and you want to prove yourself to the town. And now we can't mate because we have to make it look like Levi and I are fighting over you." I had thought I was fine with the wait. I truly had. But hearing her put me off to help Levi was too much for my Jade pride. "How many other excuses are there going to be before you tell me I'm not the one you want?"

"How can you say that? After everything we've done together, after that night in the woods? How can you think I'm stringing you along?"

Good questions. All of them. We weren't mated yet. That was all I had to go by. My intuition couldn't be ignored. She had readily accepted the extra delay Memphis and Levi caused. She was hunting Camden, but after seeing how I dealt with Wayne, she still didn't trust me or the town to take her seriously.

"Remember when I thought you were giving me the 'it's not you, it's me' speech?" I asked.

The tension in her body eased, but confusion rolled over her face. "Yeah."

"I'm giving you the 'it's you, not me' talk." I pushed a hand through my hair as I made sense of my feelings enough to verbalize them. "There's always a reason, Brighton. In the end, it doesn't matter what that reason is. You don't want to mate me. Maybe you like me. Maybe you feel more for me. But for whatever reason, we're stuck in stasis."

"You know the reasons, and I think they're all valid and important."

Nodding, I said, "And you can feel that way. I can also feel differently. I've done a lot of work on myself. I lived under tyrants, and I was supposed to be nothing but another one of them. I'm not. My brother's not, and my sister is not. I'm proud of that. I've walked around long enough, speaking and living and treating people differently than them. I've proved myself. And I don't feel the need to keep doing it. But you do. And maybe that's a journey you need to take alone."

She recoiled. Her arms dropped to her sides. "Are you..."

I rubbed the back of my neck. Part of this conversation resonated as the right thing to do. But my decision weighed heavy on my shoulders, like an angel whispering in my ear, *are you sure?* "I don't know. I've fallen for you, Bright. As soon as I saw you. But I never thought it would turn out like this. I got you to trust me. That's no small feat. But the rest of your journey might not include me."

"All because I want to wait longer when you've been here seven months?" Her tone landed flat against the walls of the bay.

"I don't know. I'm going to be honest. I've never been anything but honest. All I know is that this"—I waggled a finger between the two of us—"isn't working for me anymore."

"You're leaving?"

"I'll bring my things back to my house and stay there with Lachlan. I'm not going anywhere. I said I would finish the library." I couldn't stop the disgusted sound that came out of my throat. "Guess that'll make everything seem more realistic, huh?"

She stared at me, her expression half-bewildered. I couldn't interpret the other half. Anger? Hurt? I no longer trusted that I could read her.

"Okay," was all she said as she spun and took the stairs two at a time, crashing out the door just as hard as she entered.

I sank into a squat and put a knee on the floor. I buried my face in my hands, regretting how all this had played out. Did I wish I had stayed in Jade Hills, found another building to renovate and lived the next couple of years until I was forced to find a mate who could stand me for another forty or fifty years?

The door squeaked open. My traitorous heart leaped, hope surging that Brighton was coming back to tell me that I had it all wrong, that I had her all wrong. But Lachlan studied me from the doorway.

"I guess I don't need to ask how it went," he said as he took the stairs down.

"We're going to be roommates again." The story spilled out of me. It might not be my place to tell him what was going on with the Peridot siblings, but I needed Lachlan to know everything. I needed to know if I had let my pride get away from me and made a horrible decision.

He thought about what I had said for several minutes. Another byproduct of growing up the way we had. We'd seen the horrible outcome of acting rashly and impulsively. Lachlan had become the most deliberate decision maker I had ever met.

"You did the right thing," he said.

His confirmation didn't soothe me as I hoped it would. "It doesn't feel like it."

"If she wanted to mate you, she'd do it. She has feelings for you, that's obvious. But something is holding her back, and it has everything to do with her and not with you."

"I feel like I gave her an ultimatum. We all have an ultimatum at a certain age, and she's only twenty-three."

"Exactly. She's young. If she's not ready to mate, she's not ready. But you only have a couple years left. You can either spend them at her side, waiting, or you can get on with your life. There's still a chance you'll find someone who will fall for you as hard as you fall for them."

But it was all wrong. I didn't want someone else. I wanted her.

My stomach was churning. The only thing I was grateful for was that I was going no farther than the house next door. If I had said I was leaving Garnet River, I wasn't sure I could follow through.

"I thought she felt the same for me." My voice came out rough.

He rested a hand on my shoulder. "You can't predict or assume how someone else feels unless they tell you." The heaviness in his words came from experience. I didn't know the story between him and Indy, but I knew their relationship wasn't a happy one.

"I'm sorry."

He dropped his hand. "We're not talking about me." But the conversation was bringing up his baggage.

"I should go get my shit out of her house while she's at work." Some might claim I was a coward, but I knew I had hurt Brighton. I had no desire to make her feel worse by having her hold the door for me like she had when I moved in. Nor did I care to torture myself in her presence.

I'd be better off leaving. But that was the last thing I

would make myself do. Taking a time-out from Brighton was hard enough.

BRIGHTON

"IS MY BROTHER BEING AN ASSHOLE?" Venus's indignant tone almost made me smile. There was no grinning going on in my life these days.

"No. He's being..." Levelheaded. Sensible. Using tough love against me. I thought I was falling in love. I thought he felt the same. But a male in love wouldn't leave his female just because she wasn't making them official. "As reasonable as can be, I guess."

"Do you agree with what he did?" True curiosity came through in her voice. She had been willing to jump all over her brother for me, and here I was, grudgingly admitting that maybe he was on to something.

"I can understand why he's upset. Did he talk to you?"

"He's ignoring his big sister's calls. I got the details out of Lachlan, but I doubt he shared them all."

I leaned back in my chair, resting my head on the back and stared at the tiled ceiling of my office. The door was closed, and no one else was in the building but Selma. I let the story spill out, every detail of our argument. Was I betraying his confidence?

Maybe this was what it was like between friends. Venus had been my first real friend after the death of my family. All the other kids my age had drifted away, unsure of how to treat me now that I was an orphan ruler with the constant vigil of Selma. Their distance likely had something to do with Camden and his family.

"I have things I need to do first," I ended with. "As simple as that."

"Both reasons are valid." There was a *but* that she didn't utter.

"Except?"

She let out a resigned sigh. "Except they could also be considered excuses. Look, we all know this was thrust upon you. You're young, you're getting your feet under you after last year, and you have an unresolved challenge. Deacon and Lachlan considered all that when they shoved Ronan in your direction, but they don't *know*."

I worried my lower lip, considering what she said. They couldn't know what it was like to be me, but they had their own challenges. "Do I even know?"

"Ronan senses that you don't," she said softly.

I squeezed my eyelids shut as hot tears pricked the backs of my eyes. All I knew was that I was back to being lonely. The fleeting time I spent with Ronan was like a forbidden dream that had unfolded in front of me. An image that showed me something I wasn't meant to have.

What had I done to deserve the torture of experiencing that level of bliss only to have it yanked away?

I forced my eyes open and straightened in my chair. There was a time this level of pity party almost took me down. I hadn't wanted to leave the house. Selma had wrestled me into my clothing and shoved me out the door to go to school. All I had wanted to do was curl into a ball and huddle in the corner. No good had come from continuing my life without my parents and my sister, so what was the point?

But Selma had out-stubborned me, and I forged ahead. Only to end up in the same room, wishing I could hide in that corner until the universe deemed me deserving enough of happiness.

I would charge ahead, one foot in front of the other. This life wasn't about me. That was the first lesson I'd had to learn. Being left to take over was my burden to shoulder. My parents hadn't brought me along on that fateful trip for a reason. My sister had been getting introduced to other clans. She had met Memphis, Maverick, and Levi that day. Then the Millers ambushed them and set their car on fire, making it look like an accident.

Perhaps I had been left in Garnet River because they sensed I would be needed. I was the ruler, and I would act like it. The fleeting happiness I experienced would be solder for my resolve.

"Either way, it's done. I have plenty to deal with, and if I don't mate until I'm thirty-four and three hundred and sixty-four days old, then so be it."

"Ultimately, we all want what's best for you." She hesitated. "But sometimes, we don't see clearly for ourselves what that really is."

Venus had been bumping up against her thirty-fifth birthday when a much younger Penn asked her to take him as her mate. She fled Jade Hills to Minneapolis to stay with Steel's human mate Avril. When Penn and Steel came to find her, Venus was almost killed by the Millers before she accepted Penn. And meanwhile, Steel and Avril had been making a baby.

The two couples were deliriously happy. But Venus's circumstances weren't mine. And while it might have taken Steel months to convince Avril he was the right guy for her, they might not have made it over that hump without the baby.

They had a condom failure, but that wasn't my case.

I didn't want to diminish what my friends had been through, but none of them were rulers. None of them had the responsibility of the clan on their shoulders, and none of them had people actively working against their success.

"I'll keep that in mind." I wouldn't. I had too much to do. There was a knock at the door. "Thanks for calling, Venus, but I have to go."

I hung up, grateful for the reason to get out of an uncomfortable conversation until Wayne barged in.

"What are the Peridots doing here? Why aren't you answering my questions about the post office? And why is Ronan back in his house?"

Irritation sizzled under my skin. I coolly regarded Wayne. "Have a seat." My job wasn't to hold information close to my chest. I needed to acknowledge Wayne's role in the clan as a council member while addressing his concerns. "Memphis and Levi are guests of Garnet River. Levi has offered to mate me, but to answer your other question, I have agreed to mate with no one."

He stood and paced my office. "I don't understand. You invite the Jade here as a potential mate, and when you finally start something with him, Levi comes along. Are they both that interested in being ruler?"

As if it couldn't be me they both wanted.

My heart sank. It wasn't. I stuffed my heartbreak aside. I had to be strong in front of Wayne. "Regardless of who I take as a partner, I will be ruler."

He stopped in the middle of the room. "I understand. But I don't think you understand how the rest of this clan worries. I'll admit I was just as nervous as the others when Ronan Jade came back to town, and it was clear why he was here."

The story that he was helping with renovations apparently didn't go that far. "It was suggested that perhaps we would be a good match. Whether we are or not remains to be seen." A band tightened around my chest. I had thought we were a good match. "As for Levi, I need to make sure whoever I take knows their place in this clan."

Wayne's head bobbed, his brows drawn together as he listened. I didn't sense any disagreement, only concern about who would be at my side and therefore have influence over the goings-on in the clan. Perhaps Wayne wasn't against me. Perhaps his main concern ultimately was the clan.

Which made me wonder about the post office. "As for your other question, the post office remains functional throughout all the other renovations. While it does need serious upgrades, the structure was signed off by the contractors who evaluated all the buildings we hope to improve. But even with Ronan's help, this is a costly venture. I don't want to rush into the post office until I know where my finances stand. Kiva's supposed to compile all the information for our next meeting."

He glanced at a chair like he wanted to sit but second-guessed himself. "I understand. Just... when you do start on it, can you make sure you have Ronan or Levi with you?"

My irritation had decreased until he said that. Now it burned as hot as a match to a pile of dead brush. "I'll decide who I have with me when the time comes, if I need anyone with me."

"I'd be happy to accompany you. Even Selma."

I didn't understand his earnestness, and if he wasn't going to come out and say why he was worried about me entering a post office by myself, I was done with him. "I'll keep your suggestion in mind. Thank you, Wayne." He must've caught the finality in my voice. He nodded and scurried out of my office.

I had been wondering if Wayne was one of the council members who thought Camden would be a better choice. Then it appeared like he thought Ronan could do the job instead of me. Was it because he had watched me grow up? Did he have something against a female in the job? Or was he on my side and had an awful way of showing it?

I'd add it to my list of crap to worry about later. Same with the post office.

CHAPTER

THIRTEEN

R onan

LACHLAN CARRIED one end of the bookshelf and I held the other. We butted it up against the wall.

I stepped back and evaluated its positioning against the rest. "Looks good." I should sound happier, but the last two weeks of working sixteen hours a day polishing old bookshelves and building new ones with my brother wasn't the meditative time I hoped it would be.

The library was done.

"All they need to do is fill it with books and find a librarian," I said.

And I needed to find something else to do with my life. Brighton hadn't budged on her stance. I watched her head to the woods every night for her hunts. Sometimes Levi joined her, and I would've turned into an enraged, jealous male, but Memphis had waltzed into the woods with them.

Brighton and Levi talked a lot. And I spied a lot. Did they know I had a clear view of city hall and the diner from half the windows in the library? Brighton made her rounds during the day. She ate lunch with different shifters. She'd chat with people in the street. She was doing what I had recommended. And didn't that tear my pride in two different directions. The only balm was seeing Memphis chaperone her brother wherever he went.

The only time she wasn't with her brother was when she met Lachlan for lunch at the diner. I'd wonder if they had a thing going, but Lachlan returned to the library smelling of nothing but greasy food and fresh coffee.

I had asked him once what they talked about and he'd given me a bewildered look. *Ruler shit.* As if there was no other reason he'd chat with her.

"What now?" Lachlan ran his hand over the smooth finish of the wood. He should have gone back to Jade Hills by now, but he had taken to the renovating work like a bear to a pot of honey. Apparently my brother needed a vacation.

"The contractors aren't done with city hall." I could take over, but they were contracted, and it wasn't a good idea for me to be that close to a female who was no longer mine, if she ever had been. I shrugged, hopelessness settling into my chest. "It's time for me to go."

He folded his arms and gave me the same worried look he'd been shooting me for the last two weeks. "You think she's going to take Levi?"

I let out a weary exhale. "I don't think she's going to take either of us. She's married to her job."

"The job won't keep her warm at night. And it's a hell of a lot easier when you have some support at home." His mouth pressed into a flat line. After being with him for the last couple of weeks, and witnessing the way he stared into the distance, lost and alone in his thoughts, I got a better sense of what was going on with him. He would never tell me. But I suspected he loved Indy more than she loved him. And it was slowly tearing away at his insides.

Taking Indy as a mate was the only time he had behaved similarly to our parents. I hadn't approved, but it wasn't like females had ever resisted Lachlan. Indy hadn't resisted him either. She had saved that for after they were together.

I didn't feel better because my brother also had problems, but it eased some of the ache to know we suffered together.

"In the end, it's her decision." I shrugged.

Lachlan's expression turned more solemn than I had ever seen. "Not forcing her, or using coercion or ultimatums, was the right choice. You can always bounce back from that."

The gravity he spoke with caught me off guard. "Is that what happened with Indy?" He hadn't taken a mate until right before he turned thirty-five. Waiting until the last minute didn't worry the rest of us. He'd had his pick of females, so Venus and I assumed Indy had been willing.

"We're not talking about me."

"Do you think maybe we should?" Who else would he talk to? He shook his head just as my phone vibrated. When I pulled it out of my pocket and saw the name on the screen, I sighed. "I should probably answer, or she'll send one of the Silvers after me."

I'd been ignoring her calls. I didn't need to be chewed out for hurting Brighton. I mentally flogged myself every day. But just because my sister could leave Jade Hills with no Jade to oversee, it didn't mean she'd drop the subject.

Lachlan backed away slowly as if he didn't want to get near an argument with our sister.

Might as well get it over with. "Hello?"

"You haven't come to your senses yet, have you?"

Right to the point. "Nothing has changed, V."

"Let me ask you this." There was movement on the other side of the line like she was switching ears. "Have you only been thinking about all the reasons why you made the best decision?"

I tipped my head back and glared at the ceiling. I didn't know what she expected from me. Brighton had been keeping me awake for two weeks. I had barely talked to her since our breakup. I missed her with every cell in my body. She was all I thought about day and night. "As a matter of fact, Lachlan and I were just talking about how good of a decision it was not to force her to mate."

"He would know," she grumbled. Had I been in my own little world and not seen what my brother was going through? "But he's right."

She couldn't see, but I nodded too. "Exactly."

"But that doesn't mean you have to leave her."

I let out a weary exhale. "Venus, we've been over this." And over and over and over. If I didn't have the work in the library to keep me sane, I didn't know what I would've done.

"You've been over part of it. You think you put your-self in her shoes, but you need to go farther back."

Frowning, I switched from staring at the ceiling to studying the scuffed tips of my work boots. The new plank flooring made my footwear look raggedier than normal. "Okay?"

"She was living a happy life, humming along until her parents were taken away. Her sister was taken away. Her home was taken away. The council she thought she could rely on is slowly going away. Selma's thinking about retiring and Brighton's not sure who else she can trust. An adult can look at that and see it for the shitty circum-stances it is. But it's been happening to her since she was a kid. Everything she's been attached to has left her."

Numbness crept over my body as Venus's words sank in. From my right, Lachlan let out a low whistle. Shifter hearing meant he heard everything.

"Shit," I said.

"Yeah," she agreed. "Don't blame yourself. That wasn't some revelation I came up with myself. Ava, Avril, and I have been discussing you and her."

I expected to bristle hearing my personal business being chatted about among people I didn't know very well. Instead, relief filtered through me, awakening nerves that had gone cold at Venus's insight. This was how it was meant to be. My siblings and I weren't supposed to be isolated, cut off from all support because of our behavior. All those years we had struggled to change were coming to fruition.

I cleared my suddenly thick throat. "What do I do?"

"Get over yourself. I know it sucks to feel like you're not as important in her life as you think you should be, but it might be fear. You know she's scared of losing the clan, and she wants to help Peridot because that would also aid the clan to have them as allies. And Levi became a fast friend."

I pinched my eyes shut again. Damn. She was trying to hold her clan together. It'd gut her if she could've helped Levi and he perished instead. I was selfish. The Jade pride had bitten me in the ass once again.

"But," Venus continued, "she could be more terrified of losing you, and she doesn't even know it. Subconsciously, she might think it's inevitable."

Which made the way Brighton was struggling to hang on to her leadership more understandable. Her clan was the foundation of everything she had lost. If it was ripped from her grip, she'd feel like she had nothing.

"I've gotta go." I hung up before Venus said goodbye.

I met Lachlan's gaze. "Can you lock up here?"

"I was already planning on it."

I rushed out the door. It was time to earn back Brighton's trust. In me. In us. To get her to believe that any time together was better than none at all.

BRIGHTON

I STOPPED at Selma's apartment and knocked.

She tugged open the door, a huge smile already on her face, a touch of ever-present concern in her eyes. "Brighton. I was just thinking about putting a roast in. Do you want to stay for dinner?"

I was about to shake my head, but my stomach clenched, reminding me that I had worked through lunch. "I have to go check on the post office first, but I'd love to come back." I had been morosely eating quick food in my kitchen while standing up for the last two weeks. I hadn't had a real meal since Ronan moved out.

"Is there something wrong with the post office?"

Wayne's visit had been on my mind all day. I couldn't keep Ronan in Garnet River as cheap labor. It wouldn't be fair to him, and my nerves couldn't take the stress of possibly seeing him. Or worse—talking to him. Having to keep my distance when I knew how good he could make me feel. But he'd devastated me.

How was he handling the breakup? His clothing had been gone before I'd gotten home that day. He'd made himself scarce since our breakup. The library would be done any day. Any minute. Then what? Would he leave?

Selma watched me, waiting for an answer.

The post office. "The contractor would like to get his guys in there in a couple of days. He can give me options and estimates after he does the energy audit."

"Wouldn't it be nice if all we needed was a new propane tank?"

The tank was in good shape. The work required would be much more expensive. "It would be. I plan to hire the same crew for the rest of the renovations. They've proven themselves trustworthy." And several of the townsfolk I'd talked to over the last couple of weeks mentioned how pleased they were. A couple of the females were dating a couple of guys from the crew.

Surprise rippled across Selma's face. "Ronan's leaving?"

"It's not right to keep asking him to do work for the clan."

She folded her arms, looking diminutive in her baby-pink long-sleeve shirt and brown cardigan wrapped around her. "We can pay him." She failed to hide the hopefulness in her voice.

"I can't." My voice cracked and the familiar stinging tears hit the backs of my eyes.

She put a reassuring hand on my shoulder. "I understand." She tucked her arms around herself once more. Ever frugal, she would never turn the heat up even if the clan was flush with money. "How are the other council members dealing with the news that their offices are getting moved into city hall?"

"You should be worried about how I'm going to take it. I'll have to get used to having Wayne, Jimmie, and Kiva around." We shared a smile. "I need to find Jimmie too. He has some thoughts about what we should incorporate in the renovations."

"Jimmie definitely has some thoughts. He lords over that post office like it's his baby and we're all kid snatchers."

That was exactly how Jimmie acted. Odd that Wayne had been the one insisting on being in the know. "I doubt anyone's there now, but I'll do a walk-through while the roast is cooking." My stomach rumbled.

Selma chuckled. "I'll pick an extra-large one. I'm sure your eating habits have been atrocious." Sympathy glowed in her eyes. "I'm not too old to remember heartbreak."

"Thanks." I left before I did something like cry where someone could see me. I loved Selma, but this pain was too private.

I didn't bother with a coat. Outside, I shoved my hands in the pockets of my jeans and picked my way across the icy patches in the street toward the post office a half a block away. It was on the edge of town, butting up against the trees that circled the town.

I spotted Jimmie at the gas station, filling up a red five-gallon bucket with gas. He enjoyed snowmobiling to his kids' places outside of town. I didn't alter my course. I'd find him later. The post office belonged to the city and I could walk through whenever I wanted.

"Brighton."

I nearly choked on the wind hearing Ronan call my name. I stopped, but I took a moment to steel myself before turning to face him. Pivoting slowly, my heart wrenched at the sight of him jogging toward me. The wind ruffled his dirty-blond hair, and the tip of his nose was pink thanks to the frigid cold. His pine-covered-hearth scent reached me before he did.

I had to say something. I couldn't watch him, full of longing, as he covered the last hundred yards between us. "I was just going to the post office." As if that wasn't obvious. "I'm not holding you to your offer to help."

A strong gust of wind slapped my back. The smell of exhaust and old snow blew across my nose. Prickles of awareness danced across my skin. Was I being watched?

"I'm staying for the post office." He wasn't out of breath when he stopped in front of me, so close he could drop his head and catch my lips. "I'm staying. And if you'll take me back, I'll move every article of clothing into your house. Same with the china hutch. I saw how much you liked it. When Lachlan goes back to Jade Hills, we can sell the house I was staying in and turn the profits over to the city."

I had trouble keeping up with everything he was saying. For a moment, I didn't care. I wanted to stay wrapped in the cocoon of his body heat. "You want to move back in?" I had to have heard wrong.

He tipped his head down, just a few inches away from my face. "Venus gave me another way of looking at things. She showed me how wrong I was to leave."

"You're not wrong. You were right about everything."

"I was wrong to think that I shouldn't stay and support you. I was wrong to think that just because I love you and we had to wait to mate that you didn't love me as much."

"Wait—what did you say?"

A sexy smile graced his face. "I'm in love with you, Brighton Garnet. And I'm not leaving you. But I think that deep down, you're afraid I will. Whether it's by choice or by chance, you're afraid that I'll get taken away."

A reply stalled on my tongue. He'd uttered a fear out loud I didn't consciously know I had. But once he said it, yes, I was terrified. His leaving just proved I wasn't meant to have happiness.

"So I'm going to stay," he continued. "And I'm going to love you every minute I'm allowed to be with you."

"Ronan," I breathed. "I love you too."

His grin deepened. "You're not getting rid of me, Brighton. No matter what keeps coming up in this damn town, I'll be here."

"What if..." I blinked back tears. He caught a hot drop rolling down my cheek with the pad of his thumb and brushed it away.

"I'm sorry I left."

I shook my head and buried myself in his warm chest. His strong arms wrapped around me, and I let myself sink into him. To be with him, for however long I got him.

Sniffling, I pulled back, resting my hands on his hard pecs. "I, uh, have to evaluate the post office and find Jimmie." What he had said ran through my head. My excuses for not meeting him were valid, but were they just that? Excuses? He had shown he wouldn't bulldoze my leadership, and it was up to me to prove I was a good ruler whether I had a mate or not. "You know what? That can wait."

His sinful grin was back in place. "I know how important it is to you. Let's go take a look."

"Are you sure?" I didn't want to fuck up two seconds after we made amends.

"I understand you, Brighton. I finally get it. But like my sister said, I can't take all the credit. Venus, Avril, and Ava discussed our situation and opened my eyes."

Laughter sputtered out of me. "I never thought I'd be so glad to have others in my business."

"I thought the same thing."

He tucked me under his arm and we walked to the small square building at the end of the street.

The silence between us was comfortable, but I wanted to share everything with him. This was the male I chose. The male who made me feel as safe as he made me feel strong. "My great-grandparents situated this place on the edge of town so humans wouldn't have an excuse to drive farther into Garnet River for deliveries and pickups."

"Smart move," he murmured.

I punched in the code by the back door and pushed it open. A blast of bleach cleaner hit my nose, so strong it could singe nose hairs. Before stepping inside, I let the room air out and glanced around. The prickles under my skin hadn't left.

Ronan's brows drew together as he glanced around us. "Everything okay?"

"I felt like I was being watched earlier, but I thought it was you."

He gave me a quick wink. "I was definitely watching you." He turned serious. "Do you have a bad feeling?"

I wasn't sure. "Something's not right."

CHAPTER

FOURTEEN

B righton

I SCANNED the area around the post office. The overgrowth on the outside of the building was dried and brittle. It would need to be trimmed in the spring, possibly even pulled out and replanted so it was not so dense. As for the surroundings, trees dotted the countryside before they crowded together to make the edge of the woods.

"I think one of the first things we need to do in the spring is ripping out the dead bushes and cutting back some of the closer trees."

"Agreed. We can use the wood from what we chop down for firewood."

I stepped into the dark post office. "Don't they have a security light in here?" Shifters had good eyesight and could see well in the dark, but with the heavy blinds drawn, this place was like a tomb. "I'll have to talk to Jimmie."

I inhaled, but the obnoxious bleach stench made it hard to take a breath. Underneath the smell was... something. I couldn't take a deep inhale, but I caught a scent that made me think of unwashed bodies.

Ronan flicked on a light switch. We blinked against the light.

"The smell is atrocious," I said. "But the inside looks normal."

White letters were stacked in haphazard piles on the counter lining the wall. Boxes of various sizes rested on the floor and littered the other row of counters against the far wall. The table in the middle was full of packing envelopes, pens, labels, and shipping placards and was also scattered with various papers.

"I thought Jimmie would be a neat freak," Ronan said, wandering by the table. "But this is a mess."

"I don't know Jimmie that well. His kids were a few years older than me. They live out of town a few miles, but when they stop for gas and groceries, they ignore me like their dad."

"Is Jimmie cool with you?"

"I don't know, honestly. He was always a little aloof but not as detached as Kiva." I walked into the next room and flipped on the overhead light. A small garage door to receive packages was on the far end of the wall with the exit door next to it. To the left was a small bathroom. A pile of fabric was stuffed in the corner.

"What's this?" A pool of dread weighed down my stomach. The fabric was clothing. Old and tattered, like it'd been through a drying cycle with barbed wire. Too much didn't make sense.

What was going on? Jimmie didn't usually smell like bleach. The scent would cling to him, but he also stood outside half the day smoking his menthols. Between the fresh air and the cigarette smoke, I hadn't noticed anything odd about his scent. There were ever-present diesel fumes from the trucks that backed to the door to load and unload mail.

"Is that a pillow?" Ronan went to the pile and crouched. He put the fabric to his nose and inhaled. He ground his teeth together, making a fist in the fabric. "Camden."

All the pieces clunked into place. "They were uptight about the post office because they were worried about us finding out they were helping Camden."

"At least Jimmie."

Wayne would have a long way to go to prove he wasn't in on this. "Jimmie was at the gas station. It's time to confront him. Wayne too."

He rose. "And once we find him, maybe you'll be able to track that bastard down."

A new smell started trickling into the building. "Is that... gas?"

A rush of footsteps outside was faint, but Ronan spun and raced for the door we had entered through. When he gripped the handle and turned, it didn't budge.

"How could we be locked in?"

The smell of gas got stronger. A whoosh filled the air and a flickering light dawned behind the blinds on the windows.

"Fire," Ronan said grimly.

"Shit." Whoever did this had enough time to circle around, block the doors, and pour gas while we were inside. No one knew I was planning to come here. Unless they'd had a preliminary plan in place for when I did show.

Jimmie had seen me.

I grabbed an office chair and swung it upside down, ready to crack the glass of the windows.

"Wait." Ronan held his hand up and paused. "They're going to target the windows."

"We have to get out, or we're going to be cooked alive."

"We can shift."

Jimmie or Camden, or both, knew that we'd be stuck in here. Either we'd spill out the windows and be picked off by either one of them who could shoot, or we'd be sitting ducks. The place was too small to shift into our dragons.

Or was it? "You're too big to shift inside, but I can."

Ronan opened his mouth like he was going to argue, but then he glanced up. "The walls are made of cinder block, but the roof is nothing but rafters. Shift and crash through the ceiling. I'll be right behind you."

I undressed faster than I ever had in my life. While I was taking my clothes off, Ronan ducked into the bay.

The heat inside was growing, slowly sucking the oxygen out. Smoke was creeping in and tendrils curled through the cracks of the window in the frame of the door. I almost giggled. The energy audit was no longer necessary. An old building, but drafty, and extra heat for the fugitive asshole.

I ran into the bay, and as soon as I crossed the interior wall, I shifted. The heat affected me less as my skin morphed into scales. My dragon embraced the heat as much as it did the cold. The smoke clogged my airways less.

Ronan crouched by the interior wall to keep from getting taken out by my tail. When the shift was done, I carefully turned my big head and blinked. He nodded.

I bunched my muscles and executed a move foreign to my dragon body. I jumped straight up, like a startled cat in the middle of the bed. Back arched so my armored scales could pierce the tile of the ceiling. The building shook, but the roof remained in place. I didn't stop to think about how effective our decision was. We needed to stick with it so we could escape.

As soon as my talons hit the concrete floor, I lunged upward again. Debris began to rain down, but I didn't stop. Over and over, I hit the ceiling until I felt a give on a massive scale. Pain rippled through my back and head where scales had been bent or cracked. They'd heal. Spreading my wings, I pumped them, stirring up the smoke in the dust.

Ronan's cough only propelled me. With another mighty heave, I got some air under me and the roof shifted until it was about to collapse. Flapping my wings, I added more force. I was a dragon, goddammit. This roof wasn't going to take me out before the fight started.

The darkening sky was visible.

"I'm shifting!" Ronan called, a signal for me to stay where I was, straining against the roof. It wasn't like I could heave it over my head with no hands. Every time my wings came up, they hit exposed nails. The tips punctured the delicate webbing between my wing bones.

The energy of Ronan's shift washed over me seconds before the roof became light as a feather as his powerful body powered upward and shoved it the rest of the way off. Rafters folded in on themselves, twisting and groaning. Flames crawled up the exterior walls, but the wooden purchase they had been seeking was gone. The shrubbery around the post office was aflame. Same with the doors.

I surged into the sky, stretching my wings as far as they could go, gritting my fangs against the pain stabbing through my body.

That was when I spotted him. The dull dragon hunkered in the trees, deep enough to stay concealed but close enough to watch the pyro show. Motherfucking Camden Miller.

Opening my mouth, I let out a roar, the undeniable sound of a challenge.

I swung around, the building forgotten. Landing between the burning post office and the row of trees, I faced Camden. I couldn't talk, but everything about my stance said it was now or never. If he slinked away from this challenge, he would never be able to face Garnet River. He would finally be branded the coward he was. Even his staunchest supporters wouldn't be able to back him if he rejected my challenge.

His snarl traveled out of the trees. I had found him, and he didn't like that one bit.

I did the dragon equivalent of pacing, like I was bored with his delay. Any onlookers would see I was growing impatient. If this didn't end tonight, I would raze the woods until I flushed him out and killed him.

The echoing screech of a dragon sounded behind me. People were spilling out of the diner and running from the nearby neighborhood to see what was going on. Ronan circled in the air, but he was flanking left to meet the charge of an enraged dragon.

Jimmie. Two more dragons were behind him.

Of course. Jimmie's son and daughter. Their aloofness had been disguising the dislike.

Ronan flapped his wings wide and placed himself between me and the on comers. He glanced toward me, his eyes glowing a furious green. We couldn't talk, but everything about his look said, "Go fucking destroy him."

He was technically ordering me in front of the public, but I didn't care. I relished the confidence he had in me.

Breaking branches snapped my attention away from the magnificent dragon.

Camden had used my distraction to begin his attack. Venus's advice about fighting dirty streamed through my head. *Fight honorably until they force you not to.*

That was quick. I hunkered down to protect my belly and folded my wings against my back. The only thing Camden could get a hold of was scales and claws.

I held my ground as he charged, waiting until the last second to use a skill gifted only to rulers.

I belched a mouthful of flames into his face.

That's for the post office hit.

He screeched and reared back, bearing the softer scales of his stomach. Lowering my head to lead with the spikes extruding from between my ears, I lunged for him.

I was rewarded with another shriek as I pierced the softer flesh. I didn't stop the forward press of my attack. Instead, I used the long dragon's neck to my advantage and yanked my spikes out to impale him again.

His bellow hammered my eardrums. The third time I jerked my spikes out of him, he expected me to try the same thing, but I whipped my head up and caught him under his snout.

Camden was larger than me, and he was probably

stronger. But I had been taught by a couple of the best fight-ers, and thanks to Ronan and Venus, I had better training than Camden had gotten with his degenerate family.

A sharp, bony tip of his wing skated along the tougher scales of my neck, almost taking out my eye. I twisted and used the same tactic against him.

He miscalculated, rearing back too far. The recovery took him too long. I snapped my teeth around his neck. I bit down with as much force as I could muster. My jaws were on fire, and I might lose a couple of teeth, but it was worth it as his warm, metallic blood filled my mouth. Teeth would regrow. I didn't want Camden to recover.

He heaved me off, a strangled cry ripping from his lips. I skated on my side in the snow but immediately righted myself. Prowling around me, he shook his head as if trying to dislodge the agony at his long throat.

I scuttled closer, spitting fire. This stream had more distance and power than the last. Fire wasn't a skill most dragons had, often possessed by those from ruling fami-lies. I had rarely had the chance to train with it. Today, I would breathe fire until the furnace inside me went cold.

Screeches and inhuman yells echoed behind me. I couldn't risk looking. Ronan had taught me better than that. Camden circled around me, his plain green scales reflecting the dying embers around us.

I took a gamble and waited for him to attack. He had to be stressed, anxious. He had thought to trap me, not expecting Ronan to be at my side. The asshole had been in hiding for months, losing his socialization and likely his sanity.

But he continued circling as if we were wrestlers facing off on the mat. At some point, one of us had to make a move.

Was he trying to psych me out?

If that was the case, two could play that game. I opened my mouth like I was going to send another stream of flames at him. He flinched and ducked. I lurched for him, but he recovered and reared up, taking flight.

Fighting in the sky wasn't desirable, nor was it a skill we could practice very often. Flying itself was risky. Too easy to be seen. Fighting in the air where there was no concealment could expose us faster than a normal flight.

But I was ready to fight Camden anywhere.

I used my speed to my advantage. Despite my injured wings, I barreled into him. His claws scraped at my gut, but I clamped my limbs around him, tucked my wings in, and hung off him like a two-ton vest.

He dipped, not expecting a deadweight hanging off of him from a few talons. I flared my wings out and rolled. It caught him off guard, stealing our lift, and we plummeted toward the ground.

Folding my wings as fast as I could, I jerked us around. Camden took the brunt of the fall, his breath punching out of him. I wasted no time.

My teeth were back around his neck and I shook my head violently, like many other predators naturally do. Bone snapped and more blood filled my mouth.

I attacked Camden with everything I had until there was no more movement, and I kept going.

Finally, I released him. Opening my jaws, I heaved on the ground next to him. Blood and tissue polluted the snow next to his lifeless body. Camden's head was attached to his neck by shreds. I had nearly decapitated him.

We were dragon shifters. We had natural healing

ability, and very few dragons, if any, could come back from that injury. But I wasn't taking any chances.

One snap, and his head was cleaved from his neck. It was done.

An enraged roar rent the sky behind me.

Dammit. It wasn't done. Ronan was taking on three shifters while I had only fought one.

By the time I pivoted and launched myself into the air, Camden's body had returned to its human form. A protective mechanism to keep the secret of our kind.

My triumph over killing the male who had destroyed my family and haunted my existence was fleeting. The bright-green sheen on Ronan's body was slashed in several places. He dipped and swooped, defending himself against two attackers. One of the smaller dragons was on the ground, unconscious and in his human form. Jimmie's son. His body so broken he'd never heal on his own.

This should have been over. Tonight those three dragons were going to die, and if anything happened to Ronan, part of me would die with him.

RONAN

AGONY BURNED THROUGH MY BODY, but I was a male with one goal on my mind. Not one of these three dragons was reaching Brighton. If they did, it would be over my dead body.

Except Jimmie was older and experienced. A formidable opponent. No battle was ever fair, but I had already started at a disadvantage. Smoke had thickened my lungs before I took flight, and three against one was always shitty odds.

I had one major advantage none of these shifters had. I was a Jade. I had been raised to fight dirty and have no fear.

I blasted Jimmie's bigger dragon with a line of fire, hitting the thinnest leather of his wings and incinerating the tender flesh. As I spun around, I lashed out with my tail, hitting the second dragon approaching behind me.

The female nearly fluttered to the ground, but she recovered. Jimmie had landed on his feet, letting out a pained roar. His flying days were over until he healed. Until then, I would deal with his daughter.

But as I swirled around, dipping from the loss of blood leaking from the multitude of wounds scattering my body, I didn't find a dragon about to attack. A smaller dragon with a reddish-brown sheen over her scales slammed into Jimmie's daughter, ripping her from the air and into a dive. Her body slammed to the ground, and her head rebounded off the pavement. Dragon scales were stronger than armor, but our brains could still take a beating within our skull.

Brighton hit the female with fire and then chomped through her neck. Impressed gasps rippled through the crowd along with approving murmurs. A few snarls of disgust, but when I scanned the shifters watching us, their sneers were directed at the traitor.

I was losing altitude, sinking lower in the sky until I was forced to land. My feet hit the ground, my talons clicking on the pavement. But when I swung my head to find Jimmie, he wasn't there.

Frantically, I scanned the street. It was lined with

shifters, their eyes wide, reflecting the streetlights and the dying embers around the post office. Selma stepped forward, shedding her cardigan and ripping her shirt off. She walked as she undressed. Wayne stepped forward, doing the same. From farther down the block, Kiva joined them.

Selma lifted her left arm and pointed at a pickup parked half a block away from the post office. "The coward ran that way." She shifted, her dragon as small as Brighton's.

Wayne was buck naked in the middle of the road. "He's making a run for the woods. I'll cut that traitorous bastard off." He crouched as if he was going to jump, but instead, he shifted into his dragon as he launched into the air. Jimmie was still in dragon form, covering ground faster than he could as a human.

A short bellow made Wayne swing his head around. Brighton had already taken to the air. She directed her gaze from me to Wayne. Her eyes said, *He's mine.*

She circled Jimmie like a bird of prey, then swooped on him. He spun to meet the attack, but he'd put himself into a vulnerable position, exposing his tender underbelly. Enraged and betrayed, Brighton batted his talons out of the way as she landed on him, pinning him to the snowy ground.

More fire erupted from her mouth as she severed his neck with a single bite.

Damn, that was impressive. She didn't dwell on her kill but flipped around to face the crowd as if to say, *"Anyone else care to fight?"*

Kiva's glare jumped to the male I had knocked down earlier. "He's not dead yet. He must also be terminated. Agree?" She sought confirmation from Wayne and Selma.

Selma lifted her chin. She was in her dragon form, perched over the male. If he twitched, she'd gut him like a field mouse.

Wayne landed and shifted to his human form. His shoulders were squared and his chin up. Pride shone in his eyes when he glanced at Brighton, where she stood by Jimmie's dead human body, her tail twitching back and forth. "Agreed. Every traitor must meet the same fate as the Millers and Jimmie's family. I think our leader has proven herself." His eyes pinched at the corners and he shot Brighton a regretful smile as if to apologize for doubting her.

Brighton had done what she set out to do—proven to Garnet River she was the rightful leader.

She walked steadily, deliberately toward the crumpled male. Selma backed up to give Brighton room. Regret dulled Brighton's eyes as she brandished a talon and cut the male's neck. Blood trickled out, very little power left in the heart to pump blood.

A long sigh left her, smoke curling out of her nostrils. It was done.

I lumbered down the road toward her. Memphis and Levi jogged to the corner of the street across from the post office. They stopped to stand next to Lachlan. His arms were crossed, and he was evaluating the fight like he was going to give us a grade when we were done.

Memphis automatically adopted his stance, and Levi grinned as he took in the carnage. "Way to go, Brighton," he said.

A snarl ripped from Wayne. I tensed, prepared to tackle him if he went for Brighton—but not as prepared to talk myself down. I couldn't take a challenge from her.

But Wayne stood over Jimmie's body, his expression

forlorn. "I trusted him. I thought we were friends, but he was pitting me against Brighton, making me question her. Him and that damn post office." His shoulders sagged, and he sought Brighton's gaze. "I suspected he was hiding something, but I never would've guessed."

I felt for the guy. This whole night was going to be a mindfuck for a lot of townspeople.

Kiva lurched away from Wayne and his sorrow, and Selma stood over the male Brighton had just killed. They wore similar distraught expressions. They had trusted Jimmie and thought he and his grown children wouldn't be traitors and gone after a quick battle.

It was nothing to be proud of, but the kills were necessary. Camden's fate had been decided long ago, and Jimmie and his adult children had followed the same path. In the end, Brighton would've had to deal with them all. Tonight was messy, but the job was done.

Brighton was limping away from the body, her weary gaze searching for mine. Relief spread through her glowing eyes as she started my way. I met her in the middle of the street and nuzzled her bloodied neck with my snout. She blinked at me as if to ask if I was all right. I dipped my big head and blinked back. Then I nudged her with my nose toward the house.

She might've come a long way since I first got here, but she was still uncomfortable being naked in front of the entire town. She had taken out several traitors in Garnet River. She had earned not having to walk home without a stitch of clothing on.

Together, we lumbered down the road. Before we took the corner to her house, she stopped and faced the crowd. No one had left. They continued to watch us. She raised her head and let out a strong roar, the universal signal ordering them to either pitch in with the cleanup or go home.

She nuzzled her face at the base of my skull, and we continued walking.

With the crowd gathered on Main Street, we had privacy shifting at the base of her porch steps.

"How bad are you hurt?" I asked. My body was on fire. The cuts that had graced my dragon's hide were smaller in my human form, but still deep. A cloud of fatigue hung over me that wouldn't go away until I regenerated the blood I had lost. And I had skipped supper. I was really damn hungry.

"About the same as you," she said. She stared at me under the cloudy sky. We couldn't have asked for a better night to take to the skies for a fight. "It's done."

"It's done."

"I almost wonder what tomorrow will be like. But right now, I don't care."

Selma's voice rang through the night. She was issuing orders.

Brighton glanced in the direction of Main Street. "They know how well I can fight now. The next people to betray the clan won't be taken by surprise like tonight."

"We'll keep training. But tonight is going to dissuade a lot of shifters from thinking about being naughty." I pressed a kiss to her gritty forehead. Our skin was covered in soot, dirty, and fresh or drying blood. "Take a shower first. Eat some food. The council's taking care of the rest."

Her lips pursed. "Those who are left."

"A good way to tell that they're loyal." I didn't want to make light of the situation, but Jimmie's actions would burrow under her skin. She had trusted him as much as anyone else.

"I really thought it would've been Wayne, but Jimmie put him up to all the questions. Like he was trying to frame him. No wonder Wayne insisted you or Levi came with me when I went to the post office."

"It's always easy to see that stuff afterward. Jimmie fooled a lot of people, not just you."

Her brow furrowed for a second before it smoothed. "He did. There'll be thorough background checks on the candidates who run for his open spot." Her expression softened and her eyes warmed. She hooked her arm through mine. We were two naked individuals covered in muck. "But the vote will have to happen quickly. I need a full council so we can get mated."

I jerked my head toward her. "But Levi—"

"Can figure something out. I'll still help him. But I'll do it as a female mated to the male of my choice."

Grinning, I led her up the steps and into the house. "You'll have to tell me more about this male of your choice as I scrub you down in the shower."

Her tired chuckle was music to my ears. "I will start with the pledge you gave me that hasn't been broken and how much it means to me."

"What about if that male claims you after you tell him that?"

She took over, dragging me into the house. "I think that sounds like the best thing I've heard in a long time."

FIFTEEN

B righton

THIS PROBABLY WASN'T the best time to have sex, but somehow it felt right. Several cuts stung across my body, but my healing process was taking over. Same with Ronan. We had each stopped bleeding, we were drenched, and the water was only lukewarm now, but none of it mattered.

My legs were wrapped around his waist, and he was thrusting into me. I felt nothing but pleasure. The aching and burning of my wounds had receded as soon as his warm skin was on mine.

"Ronan?"

"Yeah," he grunted. My body clamped around him. I was close to exploding.

"I love you."

His lips were at my throat, licking and nibbling. He continued to thrust. "You keep saying that, and I'm going to blow before I get you off."

"Jade," I moaned.

"Every time my name leaves your lips when I'm buried inside you, it drives me fucking wild."

"I'm almost there." I turned my head, giving him more access to the crook of my neck.

Electricity licked my skin wherever his mouth touched. The bite would tell every shifter I came across I was his. I could claim him back, and I would. But that wasn't what this was about right now. This was about finally allowing myself some happiness. Of all people, I knew it could be fleeting. But that didn't have to stop me from spending every minute I could with Ronan.

His thrusts grew in frequency and power until my cries echoed off the walls. I exploded, clenching my arms and legs tight around him. His warm release filled me just as his teeth clamped on my flesh.

Pleasure turned to ecstasy. The town might've heard my cries, but I didn't care. Nothing had felt as good between us as this moment. And this was only the beginning.

When he removed his mouth from my neck, his heavy breathing brushed across my ear. The spray of water was turning from cool to cold. Without moving us, he flicked the lever to the shower off.

Except for our breathing, the silence of the bathroom was almost solemn.

"I'm yours," I murmured.

"And I'm yours."

"I plan to prove it, but first, I want to do nothing but lie in your arms while we finish healing."

He held me tightly to him as he carefully stepped out of the shower. Putting me down to towel us both off, heat filled his eyes as he stroked the cloth down my body. But the fatigue hanging on each of us was heavy.

That didn't stop him from swinging me into his arms and carrying me to the bedroom.

He tucked us between the covers and wrapped himself around my body. "So now what?"

My eyelids were heavy, but I wasn't ready to succumb to the lure of sleep. "Well, while I deal with the council, do you mind starting on plans for the post office? I don't think it's structurally sound anymore."

His chuckle vibrated through his chest into my back. "I'd say that's a good assumption."

"I want our mating to be soon." I nestled deeper into the cocoon he made around me. "Memphis and Levi will probably still be here. Do you think Venus can come?"

"Lachlan will head back so she can be here." Venus was watching over Jade Hills while both of her brothers were gone.

"Won't it bother you not to have your brother?"

He pressed a kiss to the side of my face. "Lachlan isn't a sentimental guy. He won't care if he's here or not, as long as he knows it happened. Venus, however, is a different story. Trust me, Venus should be here instead."

I chuckled. "I hope Ava and Avril can both come. I know one of their mates will have to stay behind." I let out a long exhale as if I could finally relax for the first time in over a decade. "We're going to do this then, aren't we?"

"I'm going to do you so hard."

Smiling, I rolled over and tucked my face into his chest. I should be mentally and physically exhausted after what had happened. I should be emotionally wiped after the last two weeks without Ronan. But falling asleep in his arms was different than before. I was different. And this was the start of our life together.

~

RONAN

I GRINNED while I watched my sister, Ava, and Avril surrounding Brighton. It was less than a year ago that I was standing in this spot after Venus and Penn had mated. I had seen the fresh-faced Brighton and thought a female like her would never belong to a Jade like me.

I brushed my fingers along the spot on my neck where she had put her claiming bite. I was hers and she was mine.

The ceremony took place in the completed library. The space was a hit. Penn and Venus were helping us outfit the building with technology that would suit the town. We wanted to offer computer classes for all ages, distance learning of all sorts, and any research materials the students in the community needed.

The reception took place in city hall and spilled out to the sidewalk. The spring weather was too gorgeous to miss.

"Ready to have everyone out of your hair yet?" Penn asked as he wandered toward me. His hands were in the pockets of his charcoal-gray slacks, and humor danced in his blue eyes.

I was wearing similar clothes to him, something I never thought would happen. I would've worn anything

Brighton asked me to, but she had said being totally naked during the ceremony was too distracting. So I was in black slacks and a white button-down shirt. She wore a long-sleeve, off-the-shoulder white wedding gown that clung to her curves and swirled below her knees. Casual, but far above our usual style.

Her black curls were piled on top of her head, and she was smiling and laughing with the others. Downright giddy. It was a gift to see her like that. The stress from Camden and his impending attack had affected her more than any of us had realized. She was still Brighton, but she was different. Confident. She wasn't constantly tense, as if she had to be ready to look over her shoulder any second.

Selma was flitting around the group, checking on guests. If there was anyone happier than Brighton and me, it was her. Not only was she thrilled about the mating ceremony, she performed it. But the real cherry on top of her day was Steel and Avril's little girl.

Deacon had stayed behind at Silver Lake so Ava could accompany Steel and Avril on the trip here. Seeing him as a new dad tugged on my heart in a way I had never experienced. Would that be me one day?

Maybe in a few years. Whenever Brighton wanted to start having kids, I would do my damnedest to get it done. But until then, there was no rush. She had missed out on so much life. This was her time now.

"No, I don't mind the company. Even if it's you," I joked.

Penn grinned. "Venus would've murdered Lachlan in his sleep if he hadn't returned home so she could come down."

"I'm glad it worked out."

"Me too." Penn's smile slipped. "Although I have to wonder if Indy won't murder him in his sleep now that he's back."

"Oh?" I hadn't talked to my brother much since he left, but it wasn't like we were always sending each other messages. We were close, but we weren't open in our communication.

"While he was gone, she was out in her yard humming."

My eyes widened. "What?"

"Yep."

I shook my head. Indy stayed home, quiet as a bunny, or visited her parents. There'd been no humming. "I hope they figure their shit out like the rest of us had to." I wanted my brother to be as happy as Venus and I were. We'd all suffered our childhood. He deserved love, whether he knew it or not.

Penn gave me a friendly slap on the shoulder. "It'd be nice if no one had to get close to death this time."

I chuckled, but my smile faded. While Lachlan had stayed with me, there had been an easiness about him I hadn't witnessed too often. The tension between him and his mate was causing issues, and I lived in Garnet River. I'd have to reach out more.

Steel joined our group. He was dressed the same as Penn. "Did Levi follow Lachlan back to Jade Hills?"

Penn nodded. "He was getting settled in when Venus and I left. I have some ideas that I'd love his help on with what Venus and I are working on. With him in Jade Hills, he can hook up Peridot Falls with online learning."

Memphis swaggered over. She'd been friendly with the females, but the way she roamed in and around the crowd could be taken as aloofness. She was unsettled. I might not have recognized it if I wasn't recently settled myself. "Putting him to work is a good idea. He gets into trouble otherwise." She rolled her eyes. "He might do that anyway."

"There'll be a lot of us there to monitor him," Steel said. He and Penn had talked to Lachlan and Brighton about their idea. They hadn't said more than a sentence before Memphis agreed to send Levi with Lachlan. He'd be doing work for his kind, redeeming himself in a way he shouldn't have had to but will mollify Peridot's council.

Laughter rang out from the group of females as Selma danced around with baby Hazel in her arms.

Steel's eyes crinkled in the corner. He was enraptured by his daughter and his mate. He'd changed him. A year from now, would people I knew look at me and think the same? *Ronan Jade is so relaxed. He looks happy.*

They wouldn't have to wait a year. I was already a changed male. Now that we were mated, Brighton would allow me to help financially. Thanks to the brutality of my parents, my share of the family hoard was sizable. Much larger than Brighton's. It'd be a nice change to put it toward building a community up instead of tearing it down.

My gaze landed on my mate. With her dress landing just below her knees and her white flats, she only showed a small swath of skin, but it was enough to get my blood boiling. "If you'll excuse me."

Penn chuckled. "I think I know what he's going to do."

Steel nodded. "Yup."

Memphis glanced between the three of us. "What am I missing?"

Penn laughed. "He's sneaking Brighton away for a quick—or not so quick—fuck."

I ignored them, unashamed as I beelined toward my mate. "Excuse me, ladies. I need to borrow Brighton."

"Gee, for what?" Venus asked, her tone laced with sarcasm.

Ava snickered with Avril.

I tucked Brighton under my arm. "I guess since everyone knows I want to ravish you, we don't have to hide it."

"Nope. We never need to hide how we feel about each other." She smiled at the others. "Excuse us."

"Get it, girl," Ava said.

"I should be disgusted, it's my brother. But all I want to do is cheer." Venus punched her hand in the air.

I led Brighton away. "You don't mind?"

"No, I was just thinking about getting you anyway."

Gerald and Hannah, the two new city council members voted in to replace Selma and Jimmie, glanced our way.

"Congratulations," Hannah said.

"Thanks," Brighton replied. "Thanks for coming too, Gerald."

Brighton had made a point of not inviting the whole town to the ceremony or the following reception. But the two new council members had a solid reputation and were well liked. More importantly, Brighton had never had issues with them or their family, and they'd had no ties to the Millers.

We broke away from the group, heading straight for our house. In my downtime, I continued to remodel the house on the corner I'd been staying in. We would sell it like I had planned, and the funds would go to the down-town renovation project.

I was already elbow-deep into building a new post office. Each day, I woke up to the female I loved and got to do a job I enjoyed. This was a life I could have never dreamed of as a kid.

"What are you thinking?" Brighton tipped her face up.

"How I never imagined it could be this good. And how I'm pledging to do the same for you."

"Ronan, you keep making vows. But that one you've already completed."

"It's a pledge I'm going to make every day."

She stopped at the base of the porch stairs, and we faced each other a lot like the night after the fight. "I pledge the same for you."

I rested my fingers gently under her chin. "It's going to be the easiest promise you've ever made."

———

THANK you so much for reading Ronan and Brighton's story! There's one more Jade shifter sibling who has a story and it's about the mate he's already bonded to.

WHEN LACHLAN LEARNS he needs to repair his relationship with his mate, he's unsure where to even start. It wasn't like he had good role models growing up. But then she's attacked, and they have to get over their issues with each other in order to figure out where the danger's coming from in The Dragon's Bond.

Enjoy a teaser:

The woods fell quiet. Birds quit chirping. Insects went silent. Our exemplary shifter hearing didn't detect movement in the woods around us.

We could shift and take flight to search from above where the big cats were, but it was the middle of spring, and the days were getting longer. The sun was sinking lower, but its rays kept the sky bright.

A band tightened around my lungs. I was already impatient standing, waiting, in this position for something, anything, to happen.

"What do we do?" I whispered, growing frustrated with our standoff against an unknown source. It could be two shifters having issues with each other. It could have nothing to do with a feral mountain lion shifter.

"There's nothing we can do if they're not going to attack. I can't leave you here alone to go hunt for them."

I relaxed out of my fighting stance. "I'll be fine. I can shift."

"No." He shook his head, his gaze searching the trees around us. "Something's off about all of this. Get dressed."

"Lachlan—"

"Now," he barked.

I recoiled and spun around. He never talked to me like that. My mate was gloriously naked, but my furious gaze was on his face. "I can fight. Weren't we just talking about this? I can help."

Anger flashed through his expression, but when his gaze stroked down my body, another emotion took its place. Not lust. Desire? Yearning? "You can help me by getting dressed and packing up our bags. I'm telling you something's not right. This is an unusual occurrence that seems to be too much of a coincidence on the only night I decided to take a pleasurable hike."

Oh. He thought that whatever was out there expected both of us to either stand our ground, or they wanted him to leave me behind.

I scrambled back into my clothing. Lachlan prowled the shore of the lake as I packed our sandwich containers and the bottles of water into the backpacks. After I shook out the blanket and folded it, Lachlan got dressed.

Tonight was a waste of getting naked.

"We'll head back, but I want you in front. And stay close."

I hooked my backpack over my shoulders. "Do you think I'm a target?"

He brushed the backs of his fingers down my face. "I'm afraid that as soon as I chose you to be mine, you were a target."

I frowned and turned my face into his touch. I hadn't felt threatened during our time together. Other than females insinuating they could steal Lachlan's attention away from me, I'd been safe. Protected. "Promise to talk to me when we get back?"

He dipped his head, and I started down the path. With each step, my temper rose. Part of me welcomed the attack of whatever had disrupted our date night. I wanted them to pay for infringing on my time with Lachlan.

You're welcome back into the dragon world in The Dragon's Bond.

———

For new release updates, chapter sneak peeks, and exclusive quarterly short stories, sign up for Marie's newsletter and receive my first wolf shifter story free.

ABOUT THE AUTHOR

Marie Johnston writes paranormal and contemporary romance and has collected several awards in both genres. Before she was a writer, she was a microbiologist. Depending on the situation, she can be oddly unconcerned about germs or weirdly phobic. She's also a licensed medical technician and has worked as a public health microbiologist and as a lab tech in hospital and clinic labs. Marie's been a volunteer EMT, a college instructor, a security guard, a phlebotomist, a hotel clerk, and a coffee pourer in a bingo hall. All fodder for a writer!! She has four kids, an old cat, and a puppy that's bigger than half her kids.

mariejohnstonwriter.com

Follow me:

Also by Marie Johnston

More in this series

The Dragon's Oath

The Dragon's Promise

The Dragon's Vow

Jade Dragon Shifter Brothers

The Dragon's Pledge

The Dragon's Bond

Want to try my very first shifter series?

<u>The Sigma Menace</u>

Fever Claim (Book 1)

Primal Claim (Book 2)

True Claim (Book 3)

Reclaim (Book 3.5)

Lawful Claim (Book 4)

Pure Claim (Book 5)